Night-
Blooming
Cereus

Night-Blooming Cereus

Stories by
K. A. Longstreet

University of Missouri Press
Columbia and London

Copyright © 2002 by K. A. Longstreet
University of Missouri Press, Columbia, Missouri 65201
Printed and bound in the United States of America
All rights reserved
5 4 3 2 1   06 05 04 03 02

Library of Congress Cataloging-in-Publication Data

Longstreet, K. A.
　Night-blooming cereus : stories / by K. A. Longstreet.
　　p.　cm.
　ISBN 0-8262-1397-9 (alk. paper)
　I. Title.

PS3612.O54 N54　2002
813'.9—dc21

2002019036

⊚™ This paper meets the requirements of the
American National Standard for Permanence of Paper
for Printed Library Materials, Z39.48, 1984.

Text design: Jennifer Cropp
Cover design: Susan Ferber
Typesetter: The Composing Room of Michigan, Inc.
Printer and binder: The Maple-Vail Book Manufacturing Group
Typefaces: Berkeley Book, Claustrum

For acknowledgments see page 159.

Publication of this book has been assisted by the
William Peden Memorial Fund.

To George Garrett

Contents

Envoi   1

Travels in Arabia Deserta   14

Wheat Field at Auvers   31

Don't Thank Me   43

On the Night   53

Clove Hitch   64

The Visiting Room   72

The Secret Life of Objects   90

Fleurette Bleu   102

Provenance   120

Night-Blooming Cereus   135

Night-Blooming Cereus

Envoi

In the old woman's half-asleep memory she stands on the deck of a ship. She looks toward the lanterns on the bow and suddenly, in her mind, they're hanging and lit. The water in the harbor ruffles and startles and rolls between the pilings of the dock just as it did then. It gives off a deep animal gurgle and slosh. Leaning over the ship's rail, she sees a fire glow where the stone falls deepest. Small and red and dark, it is the reflection of a man's cigarette. We're moving. We're on our way, she thinks, and the slow, clanging freighter blows its horn with morose splendor into the night and pushes off.

Stars glitter overhead. Shards of broken light float in fragments on the water. An old man wrapped in a rumpled coat sings songs of bereavement softly to himself. A rooster clucks with deep intent as the wind batters his sickle tail feathers against the bars of a rough cage made of sticks.

A barefoot girl in evening dress wends her inebriated way through all the foreign tourists and adventurers, the escaping Greek functionaries and their families curled in blankets, the nameless others one can't explain and hardly knows what to think about. The girl is simply another stray, dazed bird the war has blown off course, a remnant of some suddenly unknown time: brief, just passed. Where has she left her shoes? Where has she been in her gold earrings in the shape of porpoises, her heavy glittering bracelet, her small lamé evening purse?

"Gotta shigarette?" the girl asks, thrusting out a heavily ringed hand then moving to the next: "Gotta shigarette?"

Her eyes know nothing, seem completely devoid of expression in her thin little face bleached out like silk, her hair tangled by the wind into a thousand knots.

Someone coughed and the old woman startled, not sure whether the cough had come from the girl on the ship in the distance of her mind or the woman in the adjacent hospital bed.

A large black orderly dressed in white shirt and pants raised the head of the old woman's bed and set her breakfast tray before her. The hospital room was bright with a flow of sun—the wall that faced her almost glittered with it—but the old woman's last pain shot had left her exhausted and numb, and all she could see in her mind was the ship.

An Italian girl, thin as vapor, resilient as steel—black hair cut blunt—leans over the ship's rail, daring, joking, impossibly reaching into the black rushing water, impossibly stretching toward an occasional release of white foam vanishing under the shadow of her hand.

"Si, amore . . . ," the girl cries to her lover. His face is unconcerned. His straight form as he strikes the match and cups it in both hands is a lamppost in the dark. He bends to the tongue of flame and lights his cigarette. For an instant his hair shines slick. "Amore dolce . . . ," the Italian girl purrs. "Adorato. . . ."

The old woman in her hospital bed sighed with the memory of the brittle sound of the match striking, the smell of sulfur that the wind had so quickly erased, her memory of staring at the Italian girl who she felt, at the time, had been so blessed.

She let out an inadvertent yelp as a hot arrow of pain shot from her right jaw down through her hip. She was immediately embarrassed and annoyed at herself. She did not like to disturb. But the woman in the next bed, behind the dividing muslin curtain, didn't stir. She had woken no one up.

The orderly came back to get her breakfast tray.

"Would you check with the nurse and see if I can have a pain shot?" the old woman asked.

"When I got time, lady."

"Thank you," she said.

He took away the tray with its cold scrambled eggs and toast, the sealed disposable container of grape juice, and the oatmeal in its Styrofoam bowl—all untouched. She closed her eyes, trying not to think of the pain, and saw a series of tiny humped blisters of gray paint along a riveted seam of the deck. Each had depressed like rubber when her finger pressed upon it.

A nurse came in and rolled her onto one side and peeled the dressing off the bedsore on her right hip. The old woman lay on her side with the covers pulled off and saw her own two legs crossed and straight as a pair of sprung scissors. Where once her thighs and calves had been firm the flesh now hung acquiescent and soft. She looked at her own pubic hair, which was now gray and sparse and flat, then looked away in disbelief and tried to focus on something else.

"Would you bring me a pain shot?" she asked.

"Still an hour to go," the nurse said.

Sediment rose up through the urine in cloudy swirls as the nurse drained the urine bag into a plastic measuring cup. She flushed the IV, referring to the sting of pain that made the old woman wince as "discomfort." Old needle sites covered the creased silken skin on the old woman's arms with diffuse bruises the dark, ugly color of oil slicks. She closed her eyes to a moment of nothingness the length of a watch tick. I am not afraid. I am here. I have come this far, she thought.

"Morning, Mother." The old woman felt a hand on her own and opened her eyes to her son Robert.

For a moment it was as if everything she knew and loved were back in its rightful place. The connection was so strong between her son and his deceased father that sometimes, when she fell asleep during her son's visit then woke up and saw him sitting by her bed reading the morning paper, it was as if Stavros had suddenly risen from the dead and come back.

"Bring me the map above my desk when you visit tonight. Will you, darling?" was the first thing she asked. " . . . better not fold it or it will tear apart. . . ."

That evening when he returned with the map and unrolled it for her across the bed, the old woman saw that the islands were all still there. Scattered across the great expanse of faded blue paper, its corners made into lace by years of thumbtacks, the islands looked like small irregular rocks tumbled from a sorcerer's purse, their names hanging off them like tags in outdated, slightly florid typescript. A wreath of wave surrounded each island and shoreline like a halo of mist. Over Cairo in the right-hand corner a triton blew a tremendous blast which splayed out in fine lines and shaded billows toward the north. His fish tail, coiled in a circle, looped across the waters of the Nile. His cheeks puffed round and solid as tennis balls.

"Paxos. Lefkas. Zante," the old woman whispered the names

to herself while stroking the smooth, brittle paper. "Delos." It was on Delos that she'd heard the war news and decided to cut the trip short. "Melos. Santorini named for Saint Irene. Leros and Patmos. Lesbos. Lemnos." Yes. Yes, that's right, she thought, before whispering vaguely, "Samothrace and the Winged Victory whose marble was from Paros." A huge block of glistening stone rested between two lines of oarsmen in the hold of an ancient, groaning sailing ship. Without thinking she tried to move her hips, and the pain suddenly shot like a dart through her right leg and foot. She felt with her hand for the call button looped around the side rail, but it wasn't there. It must have fallen, as it sometimes did, to the floor.

"Nurse!" she called out stridently before she could catch herself. "Nurse!"

"What is it, Mother?" Robert asked.

"I need a pain shot. I'm so sorry to bother you. Can you ask them to give me a pain shot?"

"She's coming, Mother. Just hold on."

The pain seemed to gnaw like the teeth of a rat at her hip.

"Nurse!" she called out.

"She heard you, Mother, she's coming," Robert said. "Come on. Hold my hand."

The nurse rolled the old woman over to give her the shot, and the catheter tugged and stung at the old woman's bladder, making her feel that she had to use the toilet. Her angular hipbone stuck out like an escarpment, and the skin, thin as her own breath in moments of pain, was covered with tiny round bruises where she'd received previous shots. Some were pink, and some were fuchsia, and some were almost black. The nurse rolled her onto her back, and the old woman felt a gentle buoyancy as the shot took hold and everything in the room, including herself, became fluid and slightly dispersed.

For a moment she thought it was Stavros who had turned out the light and left. But no, she now remembered that it had been Robert. Yes, she thought, for sleep was almost upon her now, I feel it. I feel it as if I were there. I know what it is. It's the spring winds from Tunisia, the Meltemi that stirs the surface of the water into milk.

Far below the sea breaks against the rocks. The water spins and dissolves in milky rivulets. A child moves over the water. Her hair falls thin and gray as ash, wispy as ancient smoke, and brushes against her shoulders as she walks. A wide ribbon of satin sits in a bow on the top of her head like a wilted pink cabbage rose tied in place years ago for a birthday photograph. The wind blows and the ocean floats toward the horizon in small, white, disintegrating fronds. The child tosses something into the distance and the old woman catches it. Dartlike markings stamped around the button's blue rim are filled with powdery dust. Yet suddenly the button that rests in the palm of her hand, the button she's just caught, becomes an eye that reflects the sky. The pupil turns incandescent and dissolves into mist.

She lay in the dark with an urgent need to nudge Stavros and wake him up. Then she remembered where she was, that she was too weak to even raise herself on her elbows, and that there was a drainage tube in her bladder, a clear plastic bag with amber urine hanging heavy as a cow's udder on the metal frame of her bed, a stale, bitter taste like the urine itself in her mouth.

Yet everything in the past seemed so easy when one compared it with the present. Didn't it, Stavros? she thought. The way our lives fell into place, the way the war threw us together. The freighter passing as each new thing made a notation on the night. One remembered. One constructed. What remained was a feeling for the thing, a look. A glance. A sense of time and motion. That prelude to love and how it felt. The memory of a scene clipped. How each memory had assumed a shape, an irrevocable and definitive place in her heart. The strange, fading imprint of this. There was something about this. Something she wanted to say. Perhaps, if she lay quietly and thought about it, it would come to her.

Within the beam of a battery-powered light three German deserters play cards. The cards flash—lucky or unlucky as the case may be—progressing, advancing the game as they slap onto the rust-scabbed deck. The tips of cigarettes flicker in the night like ancient insects.

"Never too clever," one says in a thick accent.

He speaks English and glances in her direction to gain attention. He massages an irregular birthmark on his forehead with a thumb as if it were capable of yielding thought. His eyes are shot with cunning as they try to impress. The shadows on their stubbled faces and rough hands, the deep folds of their coarse coats, a dangling scarf, recede against the highlights from the lamp. They are an aged painting one discovers on a dark museum wall. One can barely read the artist's name, for the lights have been turned low, the guard is closing the huge bronze doors. The hinges creak and the doors clang to with a heavy reverberating echo. The German suddenly stands up. On his face is a grimace and his hands are tightened into fists.

The old woman awoke with a start. Then she remembered: the Germans had played cards and she'd sat and watched. One of them had turned to her. He'd silently followed her down the steep steps and through the narrow passage to the toilet. He waited for her when she came out and pushed himself against her. She felt him hard against her as he wrapped his hand over her mouth. An old woman in black appeared, grumbling with discontent at the steepness of the steps, and the German backed off. When she got back on deck she looked for a man to sit with, and there was Stavros—who she'd never seen before, never met—sitting cross-legged on a blanket as he read a book by flashlight. She sat a yard away from him, not saying a word. He watched her fright, the agitation of her hands as her fingers attempted to brush something unpleasant from her forehead and neck. He watched her fingers curling and dissolving in the dark, her head finally nodding gently forward with sleep onto her chest.

"Koukouvaya, little owl," he said, because he'd found her there at midnight sitting on the sea's branch, and he covered her curled form with his blanket. She was too tired to protest, too tired to ask if he needed it himself.

The old woman felt the pain burn in her hip and tried to shift her weight, clawed for the call button to ask for a pain shot, but the call button wasn't there. Then she remembered it had fallen to the floor. The sound of rubber-soled shoes repeated with insistence down the hall. There was something she'd wanted to say to Stavros, something about the ship and the night and the Germans, something about the blanket. Perhaps it was some word of gratitude she'd meant to give. Some word of thanks withheld all these years because—she couldn't think why . . . —and then it came to her. She had not thanked him because he'd never asked for it. He never once expected it. It was as simple as that.

She'd woken on deck smelling diesel fuel and rust.

"Coffee?" he asks, holding out a battered thermos cup.

His face is dark like a Turk's. His eyebrows meet in sparse black hairs above the bridge of his nose. His eyes are still and enigmatic. When he speaks, the words emerge willowy and soft. On the horizon a fleshy band of color leaks through the surface of the water.

She dreads the malignant toilet, the memory of the rusty taste of the German's hand against her mouth, the hard feel of him against her abdomen and chest. The narrow hall will no longer be deserted now but will hold a long line which never moves because children and pregnant women and the aged are always let in first.

Stavros sits cross-legged next to her and pulls a worn paperback from his pocket.

"I'll read to you poetry," he says. "Listen." And he reads: "I awoke with this marble head in my hands. It exhausts my elbows and I don't know where to put it down. And the poet asks, does there exist the shape of those who have shrunk so strangely in our lives . . . ? Those who remain the shadow of waves and thoughts . . . ?"

And she sees, as he suddenly turns embarrassed, that this reading of poetry is his way of covering shyness.

"I am Stavros Margaritis." He blushes and takes off his cap.

The girl in evening dress floats by with a heavy-ringed hand, begging for a cigarette.

"Gotta cigarette?" she asks. She smiles wanly. "Just one?" and Stavros gives her the almost full pack from his pocket.

"Pas de lumière," a thin, little Frenchman says with quick disappointment as he holds his camera up to one eye.

"Are you American?" Stavros asks.

"I don't remember," she laughs.

Dawn pours over the water and up through the sky like a tide of rushing pink paint emblazoning the decks and all the tired, suddenly rosy-tinged travelers starting to move about.

The wind between one's thoughts. That was the poet Seferis, too. The wind between one's thoughts and coming alive at the water's touch.

The hanging beads of a tavern entrance sound click, click. Clickity. Click. The child's dry, gray hair whispers against her shoulders, her tiny hands are like a baby's as they gently move the beads apart. They wave bye-bye like small, plump sea creatures under heavy water as they slowly open and shut. The sound of the beads is like a game of backgammon or draughts, the shaking of dice in a cup.

She's making her rounds, the old woman thought. That's what it is. She's making her rounds and deciding who's next. If she leaned over and turned on the light, Stavros would turn over with a pleasant moan, throw his arm across her chest and wake up, and she'd tell him how much she'd appreciated . . . —but what a strange word appreciated was. It didn't mean anything really. Not in real life. In real life it fell far short.

Light greased the bed's side rail. In the dark it looked to the old woman as if Vaseline had gotten on it and not been wiped off. The curtain hanging by metal hooks from a bar had a heavy, monstrous look. When she tried to focus, the dark was the same color as the back of her lids when her eyes were shut, that color of brown and blood and night, the way the hidden insides of one's body must look. It seemed caught around her head and neck like a drawn-tight blanket. The walls closed in around her, then slowly retracted and disappeared back. The world was a serpent's mouth, the night dense as pitch. If she moved an inch she would be blown away like ash. A voice from the distance shifted softly forward on small running feet, a rustle of breath or some sort of movement of cloth, then contracted and dissolved back. Perhaps it was a child visiting another patient and running in the hall. Perhaps it had come from outside and was only a pigeon ruffling its feathers as it rearranged them before flying off. Or perhaps it came from the waves—or the ship.

But there's something I need to say, she thought in protest. Just wait a moment, wait a moment and listen, let me say it. I won't be long. Have patience—please—and let me say it. She raised her unseen fragile arms in the dark as if to quiet the multitudes milling about. The IV needle pulled and stung in her wrist. Perhaps she'd pulled it out, for when she lowered her arms, the sheet under her hand felt wet. A bedpan clanged, and down the hall in the distance a toilet flushed. Whatever she'd wanted to say had fallen away from her, slippery and inaccessible, into the dark. Yet somewhere in the distance—maybe still hovering over the bed—were her thoughts. The little girl with her pink satin bow. The blue button that was really an eye in her own aged fist. The freighter moving like a shadow away from the storm of war in the dark. The old woman grabbed the side rail on her hospital bed and feebly shook it. It made a small but definitive clanging sound which echoed like a spoon against a silver cup. Somewhere was her life, the sable-fine brush of it. The morning they'd met, their wedding day, their first argument, the making up. Robert and the baby girl she'd lost. As well as those things of minute inconsequence that had been hers only through glance or thought. A splinter of glass in the dust, a wind-ripped rope on the peg of a door, a thumb-shaped shell with a bore hole that she'd hung by a string around her neck. The poet Seferis had written that the sea was green and without luster. The breast of a slain peacock. That it received us like time without an opening in it. Stavros had handed her coffee in a battered metal thermos cup. She had wanted to thank him back then, but there will always be time, she'd thought. Time had stretched in front of them, and he'd wiped the rim of the cup with the edge of the blanket. A priest with the altar chalice. Her heart broke into bittersweet fragments, tiny inarticulate bits, when she remembered the sudden beauty of this. His goodness. The funeral for the baby and how he'd wept. How every Ascension Day he'd told Robert the story of Christ's trip to heaven which had ended with:

"You can imagine how tired our poor Christ was when God finally took him up into his house."

"Poor Jesus Christ," Robert said. "How did God take him, Daddy? Did they drive in a car?"

"They rode a donkey. A donkey whose name has, sadly, been lost."

"Poor donkey . . . ," Robert had sighed.

Poor donkey, the old woman thought in the dark, remembering her husband, who had looked like a Turk, how he had aged like the Greek that he was, bending over on arthritic hands and knees in his underwear, spreading whitewash on the threshold of their suburban American house with a massive tangled brush. In the evening he would wander, follow some young woman home, knock on her door and ask for supper. Everyone in the neighborhood knew him, and someone always brought him back. He'd died sitting in the garden. When she'd lifted his chin to look into his eyes, each eye in his leathery face had been like a gray pebble in a bowl of blue milk. Sweat trickled over the old woman's scalp as she fell into a troubled sleep remembering this.

A movement of heat like a weave gone wrong brushes the surface of the water. The air is like the touching of skin when she puts her hand out. A restaurant, an awning, and a painted sign waver in the heat. A man in a deck chair sits near the edge of the water, writing in a notebook. He looks off into the far irretrievable distance with the pretense of thought. Everything is unbearably silent. Even the waves rolling in one after another with perfect timing are completely quiet. Where is Stavros? she wonders. Has he gone off? The wind whips her hair, but the wind, too, is strangely silent.

"It's time for your shot," a nurse said, lowering the side rail with a clang to pull back the sheets and roll the old woman over, pull up her gown and deliver the shot.

The wind blows and the pilings under the dock are a forest in the dark. Black water sucks and releases. It sounds like a great sea monster snoring gently and quietly to himself. An old man sleeps and feathers ruffle against a cage made of sticks. Far up above stars spring out. Islands pass in the dark, and the wind blows from Tunisia, warm from the deserts. Stavros has a dark, glowing face. He reads poetry from a book and hands her a battered thermos cup.

In the distance, a gleaming red motorcycle waits under a tree. A leaf unrolls on a branch.

Travels in Arabia Deserta

> This book is not milk for babes; it might be likened to a mirror, wherein is set forth faithfully some parcel of that soil smelling of sámn and camels, and the ancient faith of her illimitable empty wastes.
>
> *Charles M. Doughty*

I knew her by heart from that one first moment at the station. I must have been a boy of ten or eleven, but surely not as old as twelve, because by the time I was twelve the war was over and Holland had been liberated. I remember her as she must have looked on her way to meet us: tall and lanky in her tweed coat, thick brown hair tied against the nape of her neck, and her face with a kind of isolated assurance as she pedaled through the winter streets to greet us—her bicycle outfitted with tires made of wood, you couldn't buy rubber ones then—holding the handlebars tightly over the wet cobbled streets as though any moment the carved wood might split apart.

Yet it seems I only imagine my parents handing me over to her on the station platform in the dusk. My mother holding back tears and my father with a finger like a hook under the collar of my coat—implying that he wouldn't give me up—and the girl, Marta, moving toward us through the crowd with a certain angular walk, looking away with a feigned moment of unknowing, as if, with that one tiny pretense, she could assure we'd never be caught. And her asking what my name was, and my mother saying that it should be a good Dutch Protestant name, the same as the girl's. Julian Bakker they decided.

Then a sudden gust of wind blowing my mother and father onto the train that would take them back to Enschede. The train doors sliding shut, the pungent smell of sulfur, the bitter odor of iron and cinder and smoke. The train slowly starting to move as a man and woman framed in thick window glass—who were not my parents at all—lifted a suitcase up through flickering yellow light to place it in the overhead rack, and suddenly kissed. The train disappearing like water whirling down a drain. And Marta placing her hand on the top of my head with a grave, slightly teasing smile. It is true, I admit, that some of these memories have a certain reconstructed clarity over and above the rest.

She laughed and took my hand, "You have eyes that stare like a cat," she said. She lifted my cap and inspected my hair with her fingers as if buying cloth. "Same color as mine. If my father were still alive I'd introduce you and say I found you on a street corner. I'd tell him you were born out of wedlock and were just there for the taking. What do you think of that?" Then, passing through the great brick arches of the station, we stepped out into the mist.

My arms around her waist as I sat on the bicycle's back, we crossed through the dusk of a great square and over the bridge of a wide, dark canal tight with sullen barges. The facade of a grand hotel with windows glowing through the rain rose up like candles sputtering in the dark as, one by one, each extinguished for the blackout, the streets all slick and mirror-hard in front of us as she slowed down and we came to the door of a forlorn pastry shop.

"Anybody there?" she called, beating a tattoo with her fingernails on the scratched glass case containing only three meager rolls, until a sallow woman with an apron came out from the back.

"What have you got there, Marta?" the woman asked. "You know I can't take him. I have enough. I've told you that. I already have four. That's more than enough."

"I'll hide him myself. Don't worry about it," Marta said, "You can see how reserved and quiet he is. I only came in to say hello."

"Your mother's not going to agree to it."

"My mother doesn't have to know everything. She's too infirm to go down steps without help. She can't climb into the bathtub by herself."

"If your father were still alive it would be a different matter. He was. . . . " The sallow woman searched for the right word and came up with " . . . sympathetic."

I think back and try to remember the house on Prinsengracht as I saw it that night, the sitting and dining rooms opening from the entrance hall like small dark countries with ambiguous borders disappearing into the depths, and Marta leading me to the kitchen, where a door opened to steps that descended into the cellar. I hear her fumbling for something, then striking a match, and the wavering flame of an acetylene lamp becomes manifest in the dark. Her hand that holds the lamp appears and then her face, which is luminous and soft, becomes all of her, in fact. It's cold underground in this windowless basement, but then everything was cold during the war. People's hands never got warm enough to touch one another without a shiver. Yet there's a certain boundary imposed by the circle of light from the lamp which takes the two of us in but seems to ostracize everything else.

I think back and I hear the minute sound of dry tea leaves hitting the bottom of the two porcelain cups that Marta would bring down into the cellar on a tray. I hear the clank of the copper pipes inside the wall which told me her mother upstairs was washing up. I take one more feeble step back into that time and feel, for example, the slightly rough wood of the basement steps, smell the transmutation of wine through hundreds of corks, remember the musty odor of the stacked and dusty books that Marta's father, years ago, had run out of space for in the upper reaches of the house. And I recall the sound, like a dry twig underfoot, of opening *Travels in Arabia Deserta,* its spine giving out a gentle but definitive crack. Then, it seems to me, I'm able to remember everything. I'm able to fill in all those blanks with something that almost resembles memory itself. And I see, as if it were now in front of me on my desk, Doughty's epigraph on the first page: Prosit Veritati. And I say the words, *Prosit Veritati,* quietly to myself.

I didn't think of my parents then. I suppose I had an idea I'd see them soon, maybe in a week or so after this particular adventure had passed. They'd told me nothing except that I was going on a short trip. I was to be the boy, I supposed, in the stories I knew by heart, the boy who has numerous adventures at sea with hurricanes or pirates, or perhaps climbs the Matterhorn, rescues a female child in a pinafore floating alone on a raft. When he finds his way back home, his mother doesn't know him, nor his father, though they've waited for months. It's all so unexpected. They'd given him up for lost. And he's grown and changed, of course. But home he is. You can see, in the inevitable last engraving, his mother, at the front door of their simple cottage, hugging him to her ample breast.

So I adapted to a succession of days in the wine cellar, the surreptitious delivery of tea on its silver tray, and bread, and bowl of milk, the skimpy piece of cheese the size of a domino or sometimes the slightly enlarged size of a match box, an occasional boiled egg, its slices splayed on a small plate with the imprint of ivy trailing its borders. And Marta telling me how she'd stolen the egg from her mother or gone out into the country in the middle of the night to trade a bottle of wine for a loaf of dense, mule-colored bread. How there was no sugar, and how three carousing Nazis had seen her and made lewd gestures but had been too drunk to even care about being suspicious. And I adapted to the arguments I heard through the door at the top of the cellar steps, the strident voice of Mrs. Bakker chastising Marta.

"Why else would you be going so many times into the cellar? When this war is over there will be nothing left. That wine is worth thousands of gilders. I can smell it on your breath. You stink with it."

I could hear Marta saying something soft and low which I imagined to be, "Mama, Mama, quiet yourself. Please, now, don't get upset. The wine's still intact. You only imagine it on my breath."

Which was true, of course. Though the wine was slowly being traded off, none of it was on Marta's breath.

I connect that particular conversation with my memorization of the first short paragraph. To this day I repeat Doughty's precise nineteenth-century prose when in times of trouble or doubt as some might repeat a favorite mantra or prayer, though it's not a prayer at all, but the beginning narrative of a true and honest adventure. I recall repeating it when I left

Holland and got off the plane for my first semester at Columbia, then in desperation after my first wife left, two years later saying it again the night I met my present wife. It's Doughty's recounting after he had come down from Damascus with the pilgrim caravan, and this is how I remember it:

"A new voice hailed me of an old friend when I paced again in the long street of Damascus which is called straight; and suddenly taking me wondering by the hand, tell me, said he, since thou art here again in the peace and assurance of Allah, and whilst we walk towards the new blossoming orchards full of the sweet spring as the Garden of God, what moved thee or how couldest thou take such journeys into the fanatic Arabia?"

Then the long caravan of the Haj, winding its way across the deserts, is opened to me, and my present circumstances, whatever they many be, seem to disappear in Doughty's elevated words and precise tone, and, for a long moment before the world comes back, we are riding next to each other, bowing at each long, stalking camel's step over the endless sands toward Mecca.

And I hear Marta's hushed voice asking, "And how long was the caravan, Julian?"

And I hear myself answering in the lamplight, "Hundreds of kilometers, Marta. A never-ending river of camels, pilgrims on foot, the rich in litters, and Persians who had already traveled for months before joining the Haj in Damascus."

Or the voice of Mrs. Bakker on a completely different day explaining something to Marta, who was still in the kitchen eating breakfast.

"You must cut the ends. Then put each stem in by itself. Otherwise they will not stand upright. Some things one knows from birth, Marta. From birth."

"Yes, yes," Marta says.

"It is knowing, without being told, good wine from bad, how to press linen flat. That sort of thing. When it will rain or who to open the door to."

"Yes, of course, Mama," Marta says impatiently. "But you're not listening to me about this thing. That's not what I meant."

The book is as thick as the length of my forefinger, 1,368 pages. It's bound in red leather stained with time and the cellar and irregular smudged markings that have bled into it so that its antique color can hardly be called red.

"There is every year a new stirring of this goodly Oriental city in the days before the Haj," Doughty writes. "Already there come by the streets, passing daily forth, the akkâms with the swaggering litters mounted high upon the tall pilgrim camels. They are the Haj camel drivers, and upon the silent great shuffle-footed beasts, they hold insolently their paths through the narrow bazaars. The mukowwems are weathered men of the road. It is written in their hard faces that they are overcomers of the evil by the evil, and are able to deal in the long desert way with the perfidy of the elvish Beduins. . . ."

And before long I know it must be night and Mrs. Bakker gone to bed, because I hear Marta at the top of the cellar steps opening the door. And down she slowly comes, her legs and skirt and waist following after her careful feet, and I hold the lamp to light her way, and the dark glitters on the worn brick walls as if they were coal. As if the caravan had stopped to rest for the night and we, descending from our camels, had looked up into the desert sky suddenly cold with stars, and I tell her about the strangers from faraway provinces passing through the bazaars and their unusual speech and clothing, some from Asia Minor, wearing white turbans that weigh twice as much as their heads.

"Perhaps they carry their belongings in them. Like you," Marta laughs, "carrying everything you own on your head."

"The poorest pilgrims wander in the streets looking for bread, Marta. Almost every house has someone in the caravan going to Mecca."

"When the Germans come and get us, you can wrap a towel around your head and tell them you're a sheik on the way to the holy land."

The tea leaves settle in the bottom of my cup under the lamp into a loose, disorganized frown. The porcelain is so thin I could bite through it.

"The tent makers are repairing the canvas of hundreds of tents and tilts . . . and the curtains for litters," I say, no longer feeling eloquent.

"What are tilts?" she asks as she breaks a piece of bread.

But it doesn't matter and I don't know, so I say, "The curriers are selling leather buckets and saddle bottles and matara. . . ."

She brings her hand to my cheek and laughs.

But who can blame me for not wanting to remember everything that I heard from the top of the stairs, not wanting to remember Mrs. Bakker saying, "We can do nothing about the Germans. Let it be. No need to go on about it."

And Marta answering, "We should not have fought for only two days."

"If we had not fought at all your father would still be alive, and we wouldn't have them checking on us like clockwork. You young think you'll never die. It is only the old that see mortality. Besides, the Jews got themselves into trouble. Amsterdam will be an easier city without them." And then an unexpected kindness in her voice as she says, "But hard on the children to be displaced. Don't you think long train rides are hard on children, Marta?"

But when did I suspect that I wasn't the first? When did I realize that there had been others before me? When Marta opened a book of fairy tales, which I was much too old for, and exclaimed: "Ah! Michiel liked this one. He liked the drawing of the boy sailing his wooden shoe the best. Look, Julian, the boy has made a sail out of a handkerchief."

Or was it when I found the mouse-gnawed crayons and little origami animals constructed out of dusty colored paper hidden under one of the wine racks? Or finally, when Marta gave me a worn, needle-pricked doily all stretched out of shape to embroider and said, "I gave this to Kira, but I think boys sometimes like needlework."

"Didn't she want to work on it?"

"Yes, she did a fine job, and she wanted to take it with her. But I had to have it for the next child so I ripped out her work."

"What happened to Michiel and Kira?" I asked.

"I moved them on."

"Moved them on?"

"On my bicycle in the middle of the night between curfew rounds. I only receive. Someone else has to keep them."

And I would say, "Listen Marta, these are the ages of camels according to their teeth until the coming of the canines. . . ."

"Ah, you know so much from these old books," she said, looking impressed.

"The calf of one year, howwar. Of two, libny. The third, hej. The forth, jitha. The fifth, thènny. The sixth, ròbba. The seventh, siddes. And the eighth, shâgg en-naba. . . ."

"No, no," she laughed, "I can't keep up with it. . . ."

"Wafiat and mùfter. . . ."

She would rise to go up to bed, and I'd lie on my cot in the dark and see not the racks of bottles through the feeble lamp but the alleys of Damascus spreading out behind us, the passage of hundreds of litters, and hear the Persians' strange warbling like birds waking up as the sun rises, the mount of Hermon hanging before us covered with the first snowfall, white as a cloud in the mist.

It was a Sunday when the pilgrimage began. Doughty says the azure summer light had not yet faded from the Syrian heavens. The thirteenth of November, 1876. In each tent, he says, the watches are kept till dawn. A paper lantern that burns all night hangs before each entrance. A sentinel with a musket stands guard so that strangers can't pass.

And I awake the next morning hearing Marta helping her mother down from the bedroom.

"The newspaper said this is the coldest winter in twenty-three years," Mrs. Bakker says, struggling down the stairs, her voice always louder than it needs to be, for Marta is right beside her. "The houseboats have been frozen in place for weeks. The herons in Friesland are starving. Farmers are finding them dead in the fields. It's in the newspaper."

"Dead heron must be tough," says Marta, "but delicious."

"Herr Goetz is coming for a drink at six. He is not in the army. He's an importer. Your father bought wine from him before the war. We shall be decorous, Marta. Decorous."

"What's the point of having a German friend, Mama?"

"His wife died last year, poor man. He's a widower."

And I remember the odor of sometimes stale, sometimes freshly acrid, cigarette smoke as I held completely still in a packing box emptied of its books that night and Marta opened the cellar door with a stab of unnerving light, saying to Herr Goetz, "Of course, as you wish, but why not let me bring you a really good bottle." I see him looking at her dully, his eyes flat and impervious.

I would not have been able to sleep that night if the sentinel with his musket and the glowing lamp had not been outside my tent. Late that afternoon we'd seen the rising tower of a kella like an abandoned ship in the desert. We'd been riding three days without water so we were all parched and exhausted. I can still see the simple machine of drum and buckets, the shaft turned by a mule, the water flowing to fill the cistern, which, as we approached, was guarded by two riflemen. For a moment something breaks through the picture and interjects, and I hear my mother's voice come from the past:

"Put your head on your paws, little bunny, and go to sleep," her voice says, and a breath like her kiss moves over my form in the cold as I pull my blanket up.

"We were to depart betimes by the morrow," Doughty wrote, "at the cannon's word. That shot is eloquent in the desert night, the great caravan rising at the instant, with sudden untimely hubbub of the pilgrim thousands. There is a short struggle of making ready, a calling and running with lanterns, confused roaring and rucking of camels, and the tents are taken up over our heads. In this haste aught left behind will be lost, all is but a short moment and the pilgrim army is remounted. There are some so weary, of those come on foot from very great distances, that they may not waken, and the caravan removing they are left behind in the darkness. . . ."

And I dreamed then, as I slept, of a ruined city of stone with an eternity of poor nomad tents clustered around it. And a boy turning to me, his sudden wide smile and his shining glance confirming a blessing. Then his voice disappearing into the distance, and a chestnut mare, never combed by the boy but shining and beautiful and gentle, her tail flowing to the ground. The boy looked straight at me, and I saw that his eyes were diseased, as were the eyes of all the others who now came from their tents to gather around and stare.

And I dreamed of heavy sand oozing through my fingers, and a man who had fallen on the sand, a religious mendicant, groaning and stretching out his hands like eagle's claws to the passing caravan. His beggar's purse had fallen from his neck. Bits and pieces of it lay thrown upon the sand, and I saw the travelers passing on, inwardly hoping that the man's dying would not become their own. Anna mèyet, the begging derwish sobbed, I am a dying man.

Was it the night the derwish sobbed, Anna mèyet, I am a dying man, that Marta, pushed by some new importance, came down the steps carrying her deceased father's coat and elegant silk neck scarf?

The derwish had woken me. I had just that day read about a pilgrim traveler who had lifted the dying derwish to his own saddle. The derwish cried out weakly like a child. The camel rose slowly to a stand under the derwish, and the generous man gathered the derwish's bag of scattered bits and pieces, rock and shell and holy thorn, and reached it up to him, the feeble derwish all the while trembling with fear and thanks.

"Hurry, Julian," she said. "Hurry! It is so cold tonight. Put this coat on over your own."

I pulled on the sleeves of my own coat, then struggled with the other, which hung to the floor. All out of breath, she wrapped the silk scarf around my neck, tucking the fringed ends under the collar. Yet some still hung out and her hands shook.

"Marta? Where's your coat? Aren't you coming with me?" I asked.

From beyond the cellar door, I heard Mrs. Bakker's voice in the distance. "Marta? What are you up to?"

"Nothing, Mama."

"Marta, darling," Mrs. Bakker's voice paused, and then the sound of her cane, clattering down the long hall stairs in front of her. "Marta, please don't be afraid of your own mother."

"Come!" Marta said, pulling at me.

"But you have no coat."

"Come!" she hissed, pulling me toward the steps. She looked at me with fury, "Do you hear me? Walk behind me up these steps."

Marta rose ahead of me and pushed open the door.

"Mama," Marta said into the dark distance of the house. "See what happens when you try to walk by yourself? You fall, and then you can't get up."

"Give me my cane!"

"You can have it when I get back," Marta said to her unseen mother, and we walked toward the front of the house.

"Marta! I would never turn a child in. You should know that." Mrs. Bakker's voice followed us.

"How would I to know it, Mama?" Marta turned and asked, but we were already into the hall and Marta had opened the heavy front door.

Doughty said charity is cold in the great and terrible wilderness. He said pilgrims die every day. "The deceased's goods are sealed, his wayfellows in the night station wash and shroud the body and lay it in a shallow grave dug with their hands. They call any pilgrims so dying in the path of their religion, shahûd, martyrs."

"How morose you are," Marta had said, listening to me read this part the night before.

"But it's truth," I said. "Honest truth. If it wasn't, Doughty wouldn't have written it."

"But you make so much of this truth. It must be the Jew in you."

I clasp her waist with my arms and she pedals through the icy dark, my shoes, long grown too tight, skim the pavements thick with ice, and I sense, with my arms bound around her, as we travel farther and farther away from the house on Prinsengracht and on through the night, unique sympathies and virtues in the streets and neighborhoods dripping with sleet, the ravines of frozen alleys, the water in the canals gleaming like oil between slabs of ice. For a moment I thought we could have driven to heaven, but where heaven was, I didn't know.

One afternoon the Haj came to a birket that was dry. The next birket was fifty leagues away at Medáin Sâlih, but no one knew if there would be water there either. On a march like this there are many deaths. The worst is when, in the Haj's lunar cycle of thirty years, the pilgrimage takes place in the midst of summer. The sky is like burning brass, and the sand like glowing coals.

"Aren't you cold, Marta?" I ask. "Stop and take your father's coat." But my words disappear into the streets beyond.

Doughty tells about a poor man who died in a cholera year. His friends laid him in a shallow grave scooped out with their own hands. Then they heaped sand over him and left with the moving caravan. In the dry desert warmth, the man revived and sat up. He came to himself, wiped the grit from his eyes, and saw an empty world, for the Haj had long gone. Led by the footprints the way they had come, he staggered from kella to kella, from nomads to nomads, in the wilderness hundreds of miles back to Damascus, and finally arrived at his own house. Yet his family made him out to be an impostor and wouldn't greet him. They'd laid him in a grave in Arabia and mourned him as dead. Now he'd returned out of all season, and his possessions had already been divided among them.

There's no point in describing the next cellar or the family that kept me and became mine, as it were, because a year or two later the war was over. Everyone rejoiced, though it was hard for those with dead or missing family. In The Hague the Germans drove over three hundred political prisoners out to the dunes at Scheveningen in convoy trucks and shot them on the flat beach sand below the bunkers, then retreated. Some of the dead had worked for the underground press, some had held positions in the government, and some had harbored Jews.

Sometimes in dreams I see Mrs. Bakker's bulky shadow at the top of the cellar stairs. Her eyes take me in with chill and startled surprise. She sees the narrow cot covered with a single blanket, the wooden packing crate used as a table, the smaller boxes filling in for chairs, the piles of books, the enamel pot for slops unsuccessfully obscured in a corner. And I wonder what she is thinking, what—if anything—she will decide to do about all of it.

After the war, I went back to find Marta but the house had been sold. A servant next door told me that Mrs. Bakker had died and Marta had married a lawyer in Rotterdam. But the bakery across from the station was still there and in it was the same sallow woman in apron grown several years older.

"Do you remember Marta Bakker?" I asked.

She shook her head in a way I didn't understand and said, "I knew her."

"Is she in Rotterdam?"

"Further than that," the woman said, "much further than that, bless her soul."

I paid the woman for a ginger tart, which she put into a small white box tied with string, but I suddenly had no taste for it, and when I got out into the street I threw it out. I had wanted to sit with Marta in a cellar and watch her pour steaming water into two porcelain cups. I wanted to watch her cut bread into small rounds so that it would taste better because it resembled biscuits. I was older now, and it occurred to me that I might even make love to her on the cot there in the dark. I would tell her, as we lay and watched the lamp's reflection play against the beamed ceiling, that the Beduin have neither hours nor clocks.

"Listen, Marta," I'd say, "and I'll tell you the partitions of the day: El-féjr, the dawning before the sun. El-gaila, the sun rising toward noon. Eth-thóhr, the sun in the midday height. El-assr, the sun descending to mid-afternoon. Ghraibat es-shems, the sun going down to the setting. . . ."

"Enough. Enough," I hear her laughing long ago, and I'm a boy all over again. "You pretend to see the sun rise and set beyond the walls of this cellar," she says. "You know too many things for the size of your head. Lie down and sleep now. Practice being quiet."

"Mághrib is the setting of the sun that brings on the night," I tell her, "a strange town speaking in our ears."

"And what does that mean?" she asks. "A strange town speaking in our ears?"

I probably wouldn't recognize my mother and father if they should come alive and I were to pass them on the street. So much has been disposed of. But I like to think of them like that: walking down a street somewhere, going for an afternoon stroll. Yet if the Haj passed me in the dead of night—even with the moon behind it—I'd recognize Doughty by his shadow at once.

Wheat Field at Auvers

No, no, step closer, my friend. You're going to have to step up to it much closer. Don't worry about the guard, standing half asleep with his back against the wall. The worst he can do is tell us to step back. They never ask you to leave, I can attest to it. I myself would never have noticed the mark if I were always as timid as you are, always afraid to break the smallest rule, always interested in the complete picture while shunning the smallest details. And haven't they made us pay at the door? Well then, we can assume that until the museum closes at five o'clock the viewing is all ours.

And still you say you don't see it, you have no idea what I'm talking about. You see the gold leaf frame, of course. It's obvious. You say it gives a certain sense of status to the picture, telling us something about the wealth necessary to have bought it. And the small plaque attached: *Wheat Field at Auvers with White House,* Auvers-sur-Oise, June 1890, oil on canvas, 48.6 x 63.2 cm. Painted only a month before he stood in a field and shot himself in the chest. Three times he fell, then struggled to his feet to fulfill his mission and die at the inn. Three times, like Christ carrying the cross, a martyr—as any true artist is—for art.

Yet critics have said that his brushwork in this particular painting introduces a kind of order; harmony prevails. One critic has gone so far as to say that the picture is so idyllic it's sterile. To be sure, the vision is more controlled than in the gleaming cadmium orange and hookers green of the sinuous *Road Menders* in the next room, but I ask you, is it reasonable to call any Van Gogh sterile? Is it reasonable to accuse him, as some critics have, of discrediting technical skill? I don't think much of your—or anyone's—preconceived notions of life or art. He was a man who was unable to touch the stars with his hands so he touched them with his brush. Everything's in motion, I tell you. It's only in this motion that order is preserved. Unlike the language of the pen, what the eye sees is never static. To the eye, eternity is forever germinative, forever manifest.

But come, look closely. He was standing in the blowing wheat when he painted it, the white house with the blue peaked roof and stucco garden wall, the cloud-crowded sky are only a kind of vague, decorative frieze like a blurred reflection in a turgid stream running in a band along the top. The wheat bends in the wind; the air is clear as glass. It's wind and June ripening that give the painting that uncombed, gamboge yellow and sap green look, the touches of white giving the field compatibility with the house at the top. And I want you to see something else: I want you to see that there is strong evidence for something I've long suspected—that while he worked, he chewed on the sweet, white end of a blade of grass.

But people like you see only the expected, as if a first—or even second—appearance meant anything at all, you who assume that the ginger hue of my mustache and close-cropped beard and the hair on my head are completely natural. But I tell you, look not at the wheat but at the paint itself, the way the brush has smeared and driven it onto the canvas with a certain rhythmic force. I have it in me to do the same with a brush, though I have to admit that I've hardly picked one up since a twenty-year-ago Saturday painting class. It is no easier to paint a good picture than to find a diamond or a pearl. Yet after a day of going to galleries and immersing myself in the techniques and brush strokes of others, I lie in bed next to my sleeping wife and an energy flows through my arm and right hand into an imagined brush, into the paint caught there by the bristles, and onto the canvas itself, the way a runner's mind moves with running in his sleep though he may lie there still and distraught.

Note the mottled effect that gives a pulsing richness to the wheat as the wind blows across it. You can see these shot effects from Bellini and Titian all the way down to Cézanne and Rouault. Mind and thought are subservient, for only a moment ago the paint was ripe and fresh in its smooth, full tube, then squeezed in a good wormlike pile onto the encrusted pallet, terre verte, I would say, and Chinese white, and gamboge hue for the mustardy yellow, and the tubes lie crumpled and smeared with his fingerprints in the wooden box.

I see his blue workmen's clothes as if they've never been taken off, so loosely molded are they—like leather—to his curved back and shoulders, slightly caved-in chest. You see that same clear, cotton blue color on workmen all over France. The strength of the blue depends on how long the garment's been worn, how often it's washed. My gaberdine suits, of course, are dry-cleaned and well pressed. I'm even rather old-fashioned and carry a gold pocket watch. But his eyes are always bloodshot, a bad sign in anyone, including myself. We see like lace makers trapped in our work, separating and counting and knotting threads, day after day, into possibilities more and more desperate.

But I see that this intimacy, this talking about my own interior, puts you off. The fact that I've abandoned my cigars for a dark burl pipe and carry the tobacco in a square of white crumpled paper, as he did, instead of a pouch. That I peruse used book shops for old French paperbacks whose unread pages must be slit apart. Francois Raspail's *Annuare de la Santé*, for example, lies at this very moment on my bedside table. I feel you're a good enough friend that I can tell you that I've started—every two weeks or so—to visit a prostitute. And I don't shun disease. One must learn to suffer without complaint and abide pain without reluctance. It is thus—from pain—that pearls are born, a product of the oyster's sickness. It was Van Gogh who taught me all this, my friend, and another lesson, too: one pays for even the smallest success. Nietzsche, for example, believed that mutilation of one organ caused unusual development in another, that a particular mutilation was often the origin of a salient talent.

You're so positive, as you stand there listening to this, eagerly waiting to jump in and soothe with a kind word. "Never mind," I can hear you starting to say as you try to brush it all off and change the subject. But nothing you—or any other realist—can say will drive him off. He is always standing there with his paints and brushes, his bloodshot eyes searching through the bending wheat straws, reaching for Utopia, trying to form it into concrete reality with his brush. He works with such quick excitement. It's the honesty that guides his hand, the pure response. He works without noticing he's working. Life and art have become one.

Those wheat straws blowing in the wind remind me of my childhood in Frankfurt before the war when drinking straws were truly made of straw. What I would give to drink something now through a crisp, glistening straw. But then they moved to paper, which absorbed the liquid and got soft in your mouth, then plastic, which has no character at all. But you're the kind who doesn't care what a drinking straw is made of. Drinking straws today are made only for philistines like yourself.

Yet something keeps us together, doesn't it, my friend? Perhaps it's because we are such opposites. Perhaps there is something in each that looks and finds sustenance in the imagined other. And you're always good-natured; you never take my comments as insults.

But I see you've stopped listening, because, really, who but me cares about plastic drinking straws? Your nose is almost to the paint and your eyes are focused. They're buried in those rapacious but controlled strokes of green and yellow in the lower left corner. And yes, it seems to me now, you might possibly see it. Yes, I am certain, for your eyes trace up along its path as one might trace the trajectory of a minuscule rocket. It is, you say, as if a blade of grass has cut across and through the paint when it was just newly wet and soft. An artifact, you say, definitively. An artifact. Now that you know it's there, you say, you can't miss it. The paint, though now dry, of course, appears minutely flaccid as if it could still be shaped by the swipe of that blade of grass. Ah yes, you say, bringing your head up, taking your wire-rimmed glasses off and thinking about it. One never sees gnats, or the wings of flies, mist, expectorations from sneezes and coughs, or raindrops, the saliva used to point the brush. All these disintegrate as the pigment dries, yet this scratch from a blade of grass, well, that is something else, for there you see it, the tiny scuds of white and green and yellow, here and there a lump of rose madder like the broken torso of an ant, and of course, of course, you say to me, it must have happened while he was lifting the canvas off the easel. You can see, now, he's standing with us in the field and packing up, that he himself is not aware that the painting he has just completed has been changed forever into time by the swiping of a single blade of grass.

Yet we still do not know what he will do next, for he stands there in that field looking at his completed painting in thought. He will return to his room, you say, wash his face and hands, perhaps lie down and sleep, then he will go out. He walks along a road bordered with gnarled trees, his paint box in one hand and canvas in the other, the easel slung like a pack on his back, the brim of his straw hat turned up, but this particular picture, *The Painter on His Way to Work,* was destroyed by fire in the war so these memories of mine come only from a photographic reproduction. "He will choose a table in the café and write a long illustrated letter to Theo while drinking absinthe," you say. But I tell you, no, no, not at all, this is only what the unadventurous might assume from the letters, for in every life there are gaps we can only guess at, things diminished or taken for granted, things embarrassing and personal that are simply left out. Things the world would use as evidence against us, leaving us destitute of love—and quite penniless.

Take me for example, a prosperous family man, a collector, a man who can be off-putting, but doesn't forget his friends—which I know you can attest to—a man who is always talking about his own interests, yet, do you think, from our excursions to museums and occasional dinners in the summer when our wives and children are out of town, that what you see is all there is? My ginger-colored beard, for example, that seems to be the exact color of his, or the habit of imitation I have when I'm alone, the way I fasten the button at the neck of my suit and then turn the collar up?

One of my own little secrets, which I have kept from everyone, including my family, was brought back to me when I saw that he had shaved his beard and mustache off. His face had a fragile look that I'd not seen before without the hair on it, the skin loose at the jaw and neck, the usual rumpled blue jacket held with a button, a glimpse of white shirt, the stiff raw umber and yellow ochre hair that might as well be straw. Without his beard in the Bolligen self-portrait, he has become a Dutchman like any other, a porter, for example, in a train station in Amsterdam, dragging bags on a cart. His hair is badly cut, as if he'd done it himself, and only half-successfully slicked back with something rather greasy and thick. It is that dismal look in his eyes that reminds me of my own when I look in the mirror, a tension in the brow in which the muscles knit in such a way that between the eyebrows and over the bridge of the nose they make a small fist. The eyes stare at something transient and sad below the level of the canvas, just as mine stare below the level of my shaving mirror. It is this look in his eyes that reminds me of my little secret. You have guessed that I was a collaborator during the war. You suspect the provenance of some of my purchases, but I'm completely innocent where that sort of theft is concerned. No, my little secret has to do with an entirely different kind of theft.

People avoid and don't ask, and before long don't even see that look in my eyes. They assume life has a certain agreeable meaning and order for each of us. But as Schopenhauer put it, genius and madness live on common ground, and the artist is merely tolerated. He lives and works, and no one pays him any attention. Believe me, my friend, it's indescribably desolate to be forever seeking in some new museum in some new city the very peace that one's own unusual nature prevents one from finding. You who are living in settled circumstances, who stay home with your family and hardly ever travel, would do well to stay where you are. Men such as myself—made adventurers by an incomprehensible fate—lose nothing if they put their lives at stake. Even so, physical revenge against one's self is not something that one advertises or talks about.

It's the way he has of working his mouth and running his tongue, the small pink point of it, over his sunburned lower lip. The small bright red spider veins on his shrunken cheeks were why I, too, grew my beard back. Everyone does something to defend against the mirror. Wouldn't you say that everyone has a strategy to avoid the glass? The elderly who refuse to even look in it. Women with their absurd hairstyles and makeup. Animals, cats and dogs, completely ignore and turn away from it. Only infants will stare in amazement at their own saucerlike eyes and fat moving limbs. Or Van Gogh with his face shaved clean looking half away from us with frightened emptiness.

I've studied all of the portraits firsthand except the one with bandaged ear and pipe in Mr. Block's collection in Chicago. Mr. Block is rather hard to get in touch with. One has to wonder why Van Gogh would deliberately paint the bandaged left, as if refusing to ignore it. The portrait in the Kunstmuseum Basle in which the eyes are only holes of emerald green without pupil or iris, the one at the Fogg in which he's been shorn almost bald. One sees those emerald green eyes appearing over and over again—sometimes it's the whites that are green, sometimes the irises—until they culminate in

Wheat Field at Auvers 39

the picture Mrs. Whitney has in New York. He has reserved those fluorescent green eyes for only himself and his elderly mother with her black-ribboned cap. He painted her only once, and then from a photograph. One sees a touch of madness in her portrait, too. It's the eyes, of course. They're not focused parallel. They seem to gaze with delight upon a strange but delicious hell. They are the eyes of a woman who bore a son labeled mad, they are the eyes of my own mother looking back at me from my own mirror.

But now you glance at your watch and you take a step back. You are ready to make excuses. You protest, you say, "But really I must go. Another time, perhaps." You state an objection, but you will finally agree with whatever I say, for I've learned that agreement is your best weapon of defense. Yet I'm not letting you off. I insist on my words taking you with me to his small room in Arles. Surely you have a moment for that?

From Chicago to Amsterdam to Paris, I saw all four extant pictures on my fall trip—the ink drawing and three paintings—of this little blue room that looks as if it's made for dolls with its sometimes green, sometimes brown, sometimes gray floor. You've never asked about my fall trip. It's because of reserve, I suppose; you always allow your fellow man all the privacy he might require for himself. That's what one is led to believe, of course, but it's really your own fear that puts you off.

I was looking for the knife in the basin. I looked through the protective glass at the ink drawing of his room in letter to Theo—number 554—in Amsterdam, and for a moment, thought I saw the gleaming blade of it smeared with blood next to that sponge in the metal pan on the floor. The portrait of his mother with her glaring green eyes, which he has just finished, hangs over his bed. And there on the washstand, along with a water pitcher and drinking glass, a cake of soap in a dish, two glass-stoppered bottles—one for pomade and one for toilet water—is the charwoman's scrub brush that he uses to clean his hands and nails. But that pan on the floor under the washstand holds only an irregular natural sponge, and never appears in the three paintings at all. Perhaps the knife has been moved to the drawer. What I would give to be able to open that drawer. Though why I should be more certain that it's in the basin I don't know, except to say that it's where I laid mine—because of the blood. The portrait of his green-eyed mother over the bed is gone in the three subsequent paintings of his room—there's a landscape with tree over the bed instead—the ponderous burnt sienna wooden bed made up so carefully with red blanket and limp companion pillows at the head. I myself know the remonstrances a mother can impart to her son with one simple, burning look.

Wherever the knife is, whether in the drawer or under the bed, in a pocket of the hanging blue jacket, it's brother to the knife I used on myself. Well, now you have it—my little secret—and you look somewhat shocked, and all along you thought—because I told you as much—that my left ear was damaged one night by a thug in Otterlo who demanded my wallet. The lobe has been so cleanly excised, and I've done nothing to hide it. It seems obvious to me only a calculated surgery by its owner could have accomplished that.

It's murderous hard to come back to one's room at night and see a portrait of one's mother in that black-ribboned cap with that fanatic look she gets in her eyes hanging there in a frame over the bed. Days go by and I think I've forgotten her when suddenly her voice says something in my thoughts, and just when things seemed to be resolved between us—certainly I had maintained a greater responsibility toward her since my father's death and visited regularly when in Frankfurt—though my wife and children were all the way back waiting for me in New York, and the long travel, of course, to visit the paintings themselves, because a reproduction, with those awful little dots and strange distorted colors and sometimes the sides or top or bottom cut off, is simply not enough. The genuine article is important with both people and art. One might as well sit down to dinner with a handful of photographs.

What I look for is some small, rather unusual thing that will betray the man himself, the wiry mustache hair on the steeple of a church in his painting of Daubigny's garden before its last cleaning or the small pinched dab on the overcast sky in the Pushkin Museum which could only be caused by two fingers carefully coming together on the paint to remove an insect. The mustache hair traveled to the steeple on the bristles of a brush he had placed in his mouth. I went all the way to Hiroshima to see this steeple with its hair for the third—no, the fourth time—two years ago, but the painting had lost all its life for me after it was cleaned and lined and the hair was gone. All Van Gogh's must be lined with canvas and wax. The flaking is apparent with a raking light. You can see how the absorbent canvases, without sufficient ground, have drained the oil out of the paint and left it as powdery as pastel. The excessive impasto, of course, makes conservation even more difficult.

They could have listened to me and attempted to preserve the mustache hair. No one has a sense of the value of things anymore, the importance of every telling detail, the sense of one blowing blade of grass whose white end he gently crunched between his teeth as he held the grass between his lips. They simply ask to be entertained by a painting for a brief moment. Then they walk on and want to see something else. Meanwhile, the artist pays for every stroke of genius, every creative act while living in an obscurity in which no one wants to listen. And all along the pearl is the oyster's sickness just as the product of a deep-seated pain is an artist's style. I even made an explicit point of meeting with Mr. Sakuma, the director of the Hiroshima Museum of Art. Not only that but I also wrote to the conservation staff. I followed our meeting with a letter and called numerous times long distance. But you see, no one cares anymore, not even the directors.

Perhaps I've told you too much and you really must be going, but the point is an important one and I insist on making it: retouching is customary and necessary. One restores the artist's original intent. Viridian, transparent chromium oxide, can imitate the old, obsolete greens quite well, verdigris, malachite, green copper resinate and Paris. But retouching must never encroach on well-preserved, original paint. Illegitimate and presumptuous interference with the work should be forbidden in every way possible. Neither should anything, including a hair, be removed unless someone has checked with the artist.

Don't Thank Me

Sissy Martin remembered the day she fell out of the catalpa onto C. C. Hyatt like it was yesterday. The fall had given her a broken ankle and had killed C. C. This she never quite got over. Young as she was and innocent of large things, it concerned her to think of herself as the instrument of someone's death no matter how old they were.

C. C. had just turned ninety-eight and was so far removed from everything important that had ever happened to him that his memories seemed preserved and sealed with paraffin like canned goods on a cellar shelf. Except for one monumental occurrence: the week before, C. C.'s wife had had a stroke which caused her to tumble out of her wheelchair onto the hallway floor. She died right there in the hallway outside the bathroom door.

The only thing C. C. could think of was to take a picture of her with his old Polaroid camera, her chubby cheek pressed against the floor, gray hair like goose down settled on her head. As soon as the blurred photograph slid from the camera, the old woman, by a click of the shutter, had become—for eternity—preserved.

He took the ashes, mixed with gritty fragments of bone, home from the mortuary and put a handful into an empty Spice Islands jar labeled "Nutmeg." This he placed on the mantel so he could remember where it was, while the rest he attempted to work, according to his wife's wishes, into the soil around the backyard hydrangea with a wooden kitchen spoon. It was while he was digging under the hydrangea that Sissy climbed up into the old catalpa and found she couldn't get down.

It was a bright green and blue Saturday in May with just the right amount of speckled sun burning into her skin and just the right amount of breeze washing it away. After a while it was of no importance whether she could get down or not. As she rode this rough branch between earth and sky, the world became a place of infinite and far possibility.

For long, glorious moments she rode in the Derby on a horse named Quick Start sired by Man o' War and won first prize, a magnificent silver trophy, before becoming a dancer on *pointe* in Swan Lake. To a hushed theater, she danced Odette in a magnificent pas de deux, then magically became a fluttering cygnet in the next act. But the thing she liked thinking about best was flying her own plane down to Mexico, where she became leader of a gang of gaucho banditti with wide-brimmed sombreros and huge, unkempt mustachios.

"Hey down there! Mr. Hyatt!"

C. C. had a raised red spot on the top of his head that shone like a spoonful of raspberry jam through his sparse white hair. Sissy was sure glad she hadn't been born C. C. Hyatt—Mrs. Hyatt either. She thought of all the people she could have been born as, if she'd only had the chance, Esther Williams being her favorite over Eleanor Roosevelt, only now it was too late since she was already born—except for reincarnation, which seemed to her, as she thought about it, a definite possibility.

"Hey!" she yelled.

C. C., still holding the wooden spoon, laboriously stood up.
"I'm up here!" Sissy yelled.
He stood perfectly still. A look of miraculous surprise appeared on his face as he squinted into the tree's dappled confusion. The angel's voice—he was almost certain—came from the eastern sky, a portion of which was blocked from sight by the catalpa.
"How's Mrs. Hyatt? She any better?"
"She's gone up there with you, ma'am," C. C. said with respect.
"She's not up here, Mr. Hyatt."
"She's stout and in a wheelchair, you can't miss her. She's the one with the beauty curls," he said. Then suddenly aware that his wife might be listening from heaven, he added, "Pretty as a picture. Always was a looker."
"She ain't up here," Sissy said, remembering Mrs. Hyatt's precise spit curls all in a perfectly regimented row along her forehead. "But if she comes along I'll have her to give you a call. At the moment I'm engaged with matters of import. Matters that require my complete and undivided attention."
"—Sugar!" he yelled in a determined but quavering voice. "It's C. C.!"
The effort made him slightly dizzy. Tiny spots of light flew wildly in front of his eyes like the gentle but persistent motion of tadpoles in the cloudy water of a mason jar. He closed his eyes, bowed his head, and stood in resigned patience and waited as he always did whenever he attempted to look up and this particular phenomenon beset him.
Following his lead, Sissy immediately bowed her head, allowing the imitative power of prayer to sweep over her. Yet her eyes remained open and fully alert in order to follow the trail of a black ant that ran with frantic perseverance along

the periphery of an adjacent branch. She was about to block the ant with a finger, just to see what he'd do, when the sanctity of the moment was reimposed by the sight of C. C.'s bowed head.

Oahu, she thought quietly to herself, seeing the raspberry red spot gleaming like an island in the sun. She tried to remember the others. Oahu . . . Maui. Lanai. Hilo. No, Hilo was the capital. Definitely the capital. She saw it as a black dot on the edge of the island of Hawaii which seemed surrounded by endless blue water on the map of the world.

Better start over, she thought, and had already said Oahu out loud when she heard C. C.'s voice speaking with unexpected strength and determination.

"Sugar," he said, his head now up and his legs splayed to maintain a firmer stance, for the sun in the catalpa leaves seemed to burn right through his vision, "I know you're up there listening and there's something I need to say."

"Mr. Hyatt," said Sissy, "I've got an idea. How about making us lemonade?"

"No, Sugar, we'll have lemonade later. After I've said my piece." He paused, his body weak and tremulous but his mind strong now and gathering confidence.

A break in the heart-leafed foliage of the tree, caused by a storm-broken limb, let down onto Sissy's head and shoulders one solid and continuous chunk of dense yellow sun.

"I vote for lemonade," she said.

"Sugar, you know what a benediction you've been to me. You're my heart and soul. And you know I've never been a frivolous man. . . ."

Sissy was counting to ten by thousands for patience when a new idea just about struck her in the face and mowed her down. Like bats out of hell was how ideas came to her. Almost never like lightbulbs flashing on.

"I'll tell you what, Mr. Hyatt. I'll go up and find her. I'll see what she's up to, then if she doesn't have plans for the day I'll roll her on back down, and you can talk to her in person!"

"Oh, Lord, Sugar Honey," said C. C., his rheumy eyes round with apprehension. "I wasn't asking for you to roll back down."

"She says she's run out of Oil Of Olay, and she's got to come down because her skin's as dry as an old Gila monster. Says she's got to get straight to the medicine cabinet. Uh-oh! Looks like she's started to roll. Sure enough she's gaining—oooooooo wheeee there she goes . . . —whoops! She's hit a snag around the bend. Nope, never mind, she's out in the clear and good to go! Adios, Mrs. Hyatt . . . see you later! Watch out, Mr. Hyatt! Move out of the way! Those wheels are a spinning and the breeze is in the spit curls! She's rolling straight toward you! She's rolling down fast!"

C. C. raised his arms for protection. Stumbling several steps back, he fell like a scarecrow off a stick perch, and his back hit the lawn with an ugly whomp:

"Uggh!"

For a moment, he lay there dazed, all the air blown out of him. Then, after a moment or two, he seemed to wake up.

"Hold on, Mr. Hyatt," Sissy said. Whenever a situation became precarious and she hadn't a clue what to do, she'd tell a joke. This was a time-tested device her father often used on her mother. "Just hold on and listen to this: Rochester says hey Mr. Benny where'd you get the hat and Jack Benny says well I'll tell you my great grandfather gave this hat to my grandfather and my grandfather gave it to my father and my father sold it to me!" Sissy guffawed. "Get it? My father *sold* it to me! It's funny as hell," said Sissy brazenly.

"Lord, Sugar, don't tell jokes. Not now," C. C. said pitifully.

"Don't you want her down?" Sissy asked. "I thought you liked Mrs. Hyatt. I know I always did."

"Sure, Sugar, I want you down, but you're safe up there. You've made friends, you've had a chance to settle in, hang something on the walls, and . . . —well and I had a notion I might take Miss Nora Sweets to the Roundabout Club's Saturday dinner dance."

"Over my dead body!" Sissy said.

Miss Nora Sweets was no "miss" at all but a widow lady in her eighties who couldn't tell the postman from her own front doorknob. And anyway, Sissy had always had a fondness for Mrs. Hyatt. Mrs. Hyatt invited her in for five o'clock dinners of smothered chicken and chess pie, while Sissy's own mother didn't put dinner down until seven, was always complaining that Sissy didn't seem hungry, and seldom served any dessert but cubed sometimes-red, sometimes-green gelatin.

"I'm just asking her to dinner, Sugar. It's been a week since you've gone."

"I say, no way, José," Sissy said. "And if you *disobey* . . . ," she continued slowly and darkly, "let there be a curse on your hoary head!" She had just learned that hoary meant old, not a woman who would rather walk in the street than up on the sidewalk, as Kennedy Clark, who delivered the *Courier Journal* every morning, had said.

Sissy leveled her special powers of extended double-eye concentration on Mr. Hyatt.

"Okay?" she firmly asked.

C. C. breathed in deep and long, then breathed in deep

and long once more as he attempted to calm himself. Expecting to feel as dizzy as he always did from deep breaths, he shut his eyes and lowered his head. But he didn't feel dizzy at all. Instead, the yard and everything in it, the voice from heaven, the neon-bright light jumping like darts through the leaves, his sense of hope, all vanished, and he saw the picture of his life in front of him: one continuous mural of effort like that on the post office wall. Yet his own panorama differed from that in the post office, for not one of his efforts had resulted in the ripe fruits of achievement. No one—not even his wife—had ever given him an ounce of respect. It was always C. C. don't do this, C. C. do that. C. C. turn the faucet off. C. C. take out the trash. C. C. you dropped something, and he'd have to bend all the way over with his bad back and pick it up. Now even heaven couldn't see its way to giving him this one thing he had so humbly asked: one evening at the Roundabout Club dining by candlelight, waiters in constant, solicitous attendance, with Miss Nora Sweets.

Rosemary Clooney's sugar-sweet voice sang from Twyman and Bess Humphrey's screened-in porch: "How much is that doggie in the window, the one with the waggly tail. . . ."

A bead of sweat, that Sissy was afraid—in her precarious position—to swat, trickled like a fly down the middle of her back, and Harold Helm's Mexican hairless (Harold's baby sister was allergic) barked sharply three times in quick succession. The afternoon which had seemed, just minutes ago, so fresh and new was suddenly torpid and dull like a slug fallen off a leaf and curled into a formless wad after a rainstorm. Bored as hell and hot as hell, too, she thought. Even profanity, which ten minutes before had given her such brazen joy, seemed suddenly flat and colorless.

"Angel of Mercy," begged C. C., "listen here."

"Say, Mr. Hyatt? What does pree-lap-sarian mean?"

She'd heard the word on a radio show and had already received opinions from two people: Kennedy Clark, who said it had to do with the excision of female organs but don't tell a soul he said so because you-know-what would happen, and Weezie Duncan, who said I bet you heard it on that religious show it's that kind of preacher who beats himself before he becomes a monk. Beats himself? asked Sissy in awe. With what? Sting weed and such, Weezie whispered conspiratorially. Sissy was now after an informed adult opinion but suspected that no opinion would be as interesting as either Weezie's or Kennedy Clark's.

"Don't distract me, Angel of Mercy," said C. C., showing real annoyance for the first time. "It eats into my composure."

"Hey, Mr. Hyatt! Remember last Christmas? The silver dollar you gave me? I forgot to thank you." He had given her four now, three in mint condition. By the time she graduated from high school she'd have eleven. "Thank you, Mr. Hyatt!" she said. "You're a peach!"

"Don't thank me, Sugar, until you've heard what I have to say. I've thought about it long and hard. I should have told you years ago when you first asked me. But I didn't. I was too proud . . . so I'm telling you now."

Not entirely comfortable with this admission, he suddenly paused, but like a man rolling down a hill in a wagon with no brakes, he saw he had no choice but to stay his course.

"I didn't marry you because I had to," he said as the words fell out. "I know your father put me up to it, and I didn't have much choice, but I would have married you anyway. Yes, I definitely would have . . . —eventually. Yes, eventually," he gave himself an extra long pause in expectation of his wife's response, "I would have agreed to it," he said pausing again and waiting.

He stood in wonder at his own admission. Yellow and white and sap-green sun fluttered and waved and danced and the angel seemed to shift slightly in the tree, but his wife was uncharacteristically quiet.

"Yes . . . , in time I would have," he prompted.

Sissy didn't have a clue what he was talking about, but she could see that, although somewhat shaken and out of sorts, he looked brighter for this speech, and unburdened, as if gravity had been adjusted to a slightly less ponderous notch.

"Well, I never," she said to herself, spotting something small and compact on the next branch. "Hey, Mr. Hyatt! Guess what? There's a nest up here!"

"That's all you have to say to me?"

"There really is, Mr. Hyatt. And it's got eggs!"

"After everything I've gone through, that's what you have to tell me? There's a pest up there with legs? The hours I spent fishing with your father in August weather? Driving your mother to the Kroger? The humility and fortitude—yes fortitude—I've shown in every conceivable situation? That's what you have to tell me? There's a pest up there with legs? Who the hell cares? Just swat it off for Lord's sake. Swat it off, woman! Swat it off!"

"My stars, Mr. Hyatt, calm yourself. I never heard tell," she said somewhat put out, "of an adult swearing at an innocent child."

"Hear how she ignores me?" he said, looking desperately around the yard for witness. "Hear how she disparages every word out of my mouth?"

But not a thing answered. Not the bright-budded shrubs

and grass, shiny and slick-green, not the sagging wire fence, not the painted birdhouse in the shape of a little rotting church on a slanting stick. Only the square white end of a tinkling Good Humor truck that showed, now, around the corner of the house.

"C. C.," he growled hoarsely to himself, "you're a fool."

But Sissy, hot as she was and as much as she wanted to be down on the sidewalk eating her afternoon Good Humor, stayed cool.

"Jeez-Louise," she said. "He sure has his moments."

"Stay up there, vixen!" C. C. growled. "Pest is right. Let someone else push the friggin' wheelchair around." He took an angry, tremulous step and walked toward the catalpa to get to the house.

Above Sissy, the mama robin called out in shrill admonition. Below, the Good Humor truck drove off down the street with a regretful tinkling that, for a moment, seemed to contradict its own light tone and say: too bad . . . too bad . . . too bad . . . until it suddenly melted, like a Good Humor itself, into nothing but sweet, white, chocolate-coated loss.

Sissy inched, then inclined precariously over to see how many eggs were in the nest. Yes, there were four, and they were blue. Four diminutive eggs in pretty robin's egg blue. But then again, she wasn't sure: from where she sat she could only see partway into the nest. But she bet if she leaned an inch further she could see a fifth.

"Best be careful and hold on tight," she said to herself.

On the Night

Across the night fields ambulance lights glittered by the back door of the little house. Dusky shadows drifted around the ambulance. Then it drove off, disappearing into the night, its lights like so many agitated fleeing stars in the waters of its wake, and I saw that all the glowing windows had gone dark in the house, leaving it concealed, completely covered up, as if what I'd seen had only been the briefest shadow of something else.

The next morning, the two cats, one tiger, the other black as tar, jumped onto the bed and my breath blew out in vapor as the clear light of that November day cracked open like an ice tray when the ice shatters out. Gravel grated against gravel under the car's tires and the whole world, the tortuous rutted road, the definite mountains of the Blue Ridge marking the horizon, the white sky, were caught and still with impeccable cold. And I wondered if maybe I should have stayed in town. Maybe it was a mistake to spend this first year of widowhood in the country alone, but I didn't know, I couldn't tell. Maybe it was my time to be lonely, maybe I would have been just as lonely somewhere else.

Not until I walked into the one-room post office, smelling of wood smoke and tobacco and dust, and saw a handful of people bundled like refugees reaching into their ornate brass mailboxes, did I remember the midnight ambulance.

"She passed 'fore they could get there," said a heavy man to a brittle gray-haired lady as he ripped open a bill with his thumb.

"Thank the good lord he had the presence of mind to call 911," the gray-haired lady said. "Would have been just like Raymond to think he could take care of his Mildred in an emergency all by his self."

"Siren fit to wake the dead!" the heavy man said, shaking his head at the size of his electric bill.

"It's a sorry thing," said the lady. "Did he go to his daughter in the valley?"

The heavy man looked up.

"Sheriff asked him, but he wouldn't go." The man moved toward the door. "Seems like Ray couldn't believe it. Said he had to be home in case Mildred decided to come back. —See you, Mae!" and he pulled open the door and walked out.

The woman shook her head.

"Raymond sure could use a dog out there," she said. "Nobody living alone these days should be without a dog. What a terrible shame and only two days before Thanksgiving. You got a dog?" she asked.

Of course we'd hardly known Raymond and Mildred, they were a different class, nothing in common is how we would have put it, but then we'd been weekend people anyway so we hadn't mixed with anyone much. Still, the little wood-frame house across the creek and fields had always been an anchor of sorts binding the two of them together in my mind, their devotion holding fast a piece of my world on that distant, yet strangely close and intimate, piedmont rise.

Now as I drove back and saw the house, it was easy to forget that Mildred wasn't still there in her wheelchair with Raymond taking care of her. I imagined him bending over her as she lay helpless in bed. He was—I could see it clearly—holding a napkin under her chin and feeding her oatmeal from a small battered spoon.

That night when Dave's absence woke me and I couldn't sleep, the fields out the window seemed to float like an ocean, swell with the deep, and it seemed, as I looked out and saw one lighted window burning steadily in the little house, that the two of us, Raymond and myself, rode like whalers across those waving fields, two souls clinging to the top of our own infinitely precarious, swaying masts.

Yet when I saw him backing out in his old Pontiac the next morning, there was nothing—not the slightest thing—in his clear, open smile and wave to remind me that Mildred had died two nights before. It's this smile against a background of winter that distinguishes him in my mind even now, the clear look of pure innocence in his eyes, the expectation, the complete absence of guile. Otherwise he could have been any one of hundreds of old men driving at a snail's pace, the car low-slung and long, chassis barely hanging off the ground, a hindrance to anyone trying to pass him on the road.

Always with the same eager look in his eyes, he'd pull up in front of the bank or the drugstore or the post office, then sit behind the wheel and run the engine to keep warm. Anyone would have thought Mildred was still young and alive, that he was only waiting as she did her errands, that any moment she might suddenly appear on the sidewalk with a handful of mail or a white paper bag from the drugstore with her digitalis refill.

One February afternoon, as the indifferent dust of a gray snow drifted down from a colorless sky, I drove along the highway and passed him driving slow as death just for the sake of it. In my mind I saw him driving down a road like an artery that goes on and on, bifurcating into smaller and smaller vessels, until it finally terminates in the tip of a finger on one's hand. I saw the car moving like some massive, exhausted animal into a dead end of derelict cars and trash, a refrigerator on its side, a rotting sofa, or a house with a chained, growling dog and wary woman. The woman's drawn face and frightened eyes would pull back and disappear behind a shadow of curtain and paned glass, and the dog would bark and strain at its chain, filling the world with its sound.

Yet even on those bleak February days, even as the black flesh-headed buzzards floated in wide inclusive circles overhead, you could feel the year turning toward a distant spring. The winter honeysuckle came into bloom under the bedroom window so that when I cracked open the window at night, there, like a fine powdered vapor, was the odor of spring. The tar black and tiger cats' claws clicked across the invisible wood floor in the dark, and the heat came on with a low shuddering moan as I lay in bed listening for something I could only guess at, a quick deadly scuffle and scratch deep in the heart of the poplar woods, the crack of a twig or branch, a great horned owl lifting his feathers into place as he waited and watched.

Spring arrived and with it a widow lady named Virginia who'd gotten wind of Raymond's new situation. I imagined they'd known each other as far back as high school, maybe even before. She appeared the same day the forsythia exploded into swaths of yellow bloom across the sloping hillside. Within days Virginia and her possessions had moved in lock, stock, and barrel. I even overheard talk of a wedding, though

I never saw a sign of one and never saw her wear a ring. But no matter, they were as good as married with all the changes and new possessions a real wedding brings.

A delivery truck unloaded rolls of new carpet and flowered linoleum, a crushed velvet easy chair with lever for raising and lowering the footrest, and a brand new queen-size bed with a fleur-de-lis patterned headboard and gold spray-painted trim. Two men in woodsy plaid shirts replaced Mildred's ragged wheelchair ramp with neat red brick steps, stood back surveying the roof, cleaned out the gutters, hacked back a renegade patch of wisteria that threatened to take over a lilac, Virginia and her pure white head of beauty-parlored hair supervising every last bit of it.

Hot as it was that summer, it was Virginia everywhere driving one of the old cars with Raymond beside her, for Raymond's old gas-guzzler had multiplied by four, Virginia's dowry I presumed, relics from the days when the longer and flatter a car was the better. All were weathered and faded and stained with rain, eaten out like lace close to the ground, as they clustered like ships in harbor come to rest by the back door.

In one car or another the happy couple wandered down the deep briar-choked lanes to the post office or crawled along the highway to the Family Dollar Store, then drove back into town to pick up greens or tomatoes or Lysol at the IGA. Beside the immaculate presence of her white hair, her strong jaw, her determination not to let the heat and humidity get her down, and her hands firmly on the wheel, Raymond seemed noticeably smaller and lacking in intent. Except for his smile. You could see it as they passed: that one clear and obvious, uniquely immeasurable thing. I see them in their brief and hazy summer world with such personal eyes it's as if I've made them up, a fiction solely and entirely to explain something to myself.

There they were, the two of them, pushing the grocery cart down the aisle; she making hard decisions about what to put in the basket, what to take out and put back on the shelf, he with his gnarled hand on her corseted bottom. Clean-shaven as new dawn, his thin white hair slicked over the top of his balding head, his shirt pressed, his shoes polished, he looked like he'd been washed and dressed for Sunday school. Between the hams and pigs' feet and hamburger on one side and the jellies and jams and peanut butter on the other, they made their way backing and filling down the aisle; she stopping the cart to look at a price, he with his old ramble starting the cart up again.

At night when I looked out the window and saw the shadow of deer moving smoothly under the moon to bend their heads to the water and drink from the creek, the windows in the little house glowed golden, for such is the aura of a housekeeping woman in charge of a gentle, compliant man.

Yet as fall moved toward winter something changed. There Raymond was, still sitting next to Virginia as she competently steered one of the old cars down the highway into town, but his smile had become tentative and questioning as if he'd forgotten something at home that he dared not talk about. When I saw them at the IGA, Raymond pushing the cart down an aisle while Virginia spoke to the butcher about the Thanksgiving turkey, I passed him and said hello.

"Where'd she go?" he asked with a startled look.

"She's talking to the butcher," I told him. "Over there."

He turned as I pointed to Virginia's back and a look of pure contentment came upon his face. Then he said something low that sounded like, "I had a feeling she was to come back."

Virginia's square-set face turned and looked straight at him as he approached her.

"What is it, Ray honey?" she asked.

That was the beginning, in my mind, of Raymond's end, my knowing that when I drove by and saw his ghost of a face looking out his kitchen window he wasn't watching the fields and trees and sky ripen into autumn at all, he was looking hard through those trees to where the road turned in hopes that he would see his Mildred again.

All Virginia knew, as she later told me when I finally got to know her, was that Raymond had had a breakdown. What exactly had caused it she couldn't tell.

But she remembered everything clearly: what he'd said, what she'd said, what they'd both done, how that last day had moved along, and she told me the story sitting at her kitchen table three or four times that winter and spring as if telling it one more time would finally give it sense. Now what survives is a story like all stories: half the teller and half the listener, each molding it into something of her own.

"Soon as we set down for supper," she said, "the calendar on the wall caught his eye. He set his fork down and stopped chewing. Then he started in to cry like a boy who's lost his best friend."

It was easy enough to imagine Raymond's world blurring in front of him and twisting into grief as he stared at the calendar with the squared-off dates and the prophetic word: November.

"I asked him, what's the matter, Ray? Do you hurt somewhere? But he just shook his head and looked at me like he was seeing me for the first time."

"He was a gentle man. He wouldn't have wanted to disappoint you," I said, "but he'd been married to Mildred for such a long time."

"I never in my life had seen a man cry, but I cleared the dishes and thought it through and by the time I had them in the sink and on the drainboard I'd decided his crying was a gift. No one ever cried for me before. Anyone ever cry for you?"

"Yes," I told her. "My husband, Dave. The day before he died. Other times, too."

"I've seen pictures of men crying in wartime. Once in the newspaper I saw a Frenchman cry as the Nazis marched into his town, but I never did see a man cry for a woman." She thought a moment and said, "Course I myself always cry after a long trip when I get back home. After all I done for Ray I guess his tears made perfect sense."

"Maybe," I said. She seemed as sure of her explanation as I was of mine.

"I never could tell what would start him up. He'd be looking at a pillow on the sofa or the spoon rest on the stove or the sign, Virginia's Kitchen, I just put up, and he'd start in again. Wouldn't even tell me what happened to the spoon rest. Pretty thing, too, in the shape of a rooster. We bought it on sale at the Family Dollar Store. I said to Ray it was a mystery how Mildred got by without one. Every house I'd ever been in's had a spoon rest, I told him. A stove without a spoon rest's bare-bottomed," she gave me a sly little wink, "—not correctly dressed."

"Had he taken it do you think?"

"Or broke it and afraid to tell. He wouldn't say and I never did find out. But when he started to walk from one room to the next like he no longer knew where he was, when he took to just standing and staring at things or sitting for hours by the bedroom window looking out, I had no choice, I had to take him to the hospital."

"And he went without a problem?"

"Got into the car and didn't say a thing about it. This young doctor took us behind some curtains and asked Ray questions up and down about his health and his habits—did he get indigestion—did he smoke or drink—had he ever had surgery. Ray just shook his head, no. But I tell you that young doctor looked as old and tired as Ray was. First off when I saw him walk toward us I knew he'd never be able to help Ray out. Ray just sat there and said, I'm wore out. That's all he'd say. I'm wore out. Go on home, old man, the doctor told him. Have your wife put you to bed."

But of course Raymond had no wife, I wanted to say, his wife had died a year to the day. He'd followed it on the calendar, just as I followed my own calendar.

"So I took him on home," said Virginia. "He walked in the door and said he wasn't ready to go to bed yet, he'd lay down for a spell then have supper. He lay down on the spread in his clothes and fell asleep curled in the middle of the peacock's tail, the eyes of God in purple and aqua and blue tufts set about him like so many jewels set into a crown. I bought that spread from a roadside stand—you should come over to see it—gives the whole room an air. I had four to choose from. One with valentine hearts dancing every which way—crazy love the woman called it—one with purple iris, green leaves crossing like swords, and one with flamingos, but I fell in love with the peacock with the eyes of God in his tail. I took the Thanksgiving turkey out of the freezer and rolled out the crust for a pie and ate a little supper for myself then I went in to bed. I wouldn't have woken him for the world, sleeping as sound as he was. I left him in his clothes on top of the spread, and I got into bed, staying—as I had to with Ray in the middle—way over to the edge. I could feel his weight and hear his steady breathing and I knew everything was going to work out."

"I remember feeling like that," I said. "I remember feeling that nothing could ever change the life we had."

"But in the deep of night the train passed and I woke up. Seemed like the roar of train and the wheels cracking against the tracks just about split the night apart."

I remembered that the train had passed, tearing the night apart, and then the whistle had blown and the sound, like a long silk cord, had seemed to bind the night together again.

"But I also heard something else," I said. "You may think it's foolish, but I heard a sound like water underground, like the stream in its bed flowing deep in the dark."

I'd had a dream in which I passed through the shadow of deer and the tall night grass, the sycamores white as bone, the pockets of tepid air they call angel's breath. I'd bent down on all fours and touched my ear to the water, and I'd listened, taut and intent.

"No," she said positively, "I believe you. It was Ray you heard. It was Ray moving from this life on."

"Maybe so," I said. "Maybe you're right. Maybe I heard the sound of something moving on."

"I felt my way into the kitchen," she said, "and turned on the light. I sat at the table and drank my Ovaltine and looked at my kitchen lit up in front of me like a little stage set. I came into this house a complete stranger and made this kitchen—and Ray—my own, just like I did with my now-deceased husband over fifty years ago. I went back to bed, but for some reason I couldn't sleep. I just lay there listening to a screech owl wailing in the dark the way they do when they cry for the dead."

"Yes, I know. They have a strange cry like the sound exists in some separate world all by itself."

"I felt Ray's weight heavier on the spread, pulling it down, yet almost lighter in a way, and I knew he'd gone."

She stopped and, with the edge of a spoon, gently pushed a row of tiny creases into the kitchen tablecloth as she thought. Then she held the spoon still and stared at it.

"I guess I had an idea the life I knew would always go on," she said.

"We all do," I told her. "Yet underneath it all I think we really know what to expect."

"We do and we don't," she said.

That night the wind blew through the trees and fields like waves breaking against a shore as the tar black and tiger cats searched through the house, trailing after the smell of mice, their claws tapping a faint but distinct telegraph against the pine wood floor.

Yet the next morning rang still and brittle as a glass bell. The last great tulip poplar leaves had floated down and settled in the creek, and the trees now stood completely bare. Silt the color of rawhide suede lay on the smooth creek bottom. The water, after melting from ice and now running over this silt, was clear and thin as air and liquid as Virginia's wave from where she stood surrounded by the four old cars.

Clove Hitch

Bayberry and beach plum and rugosa rose, its gleaming wet branches weighed with orange-red fruit, sent roots deep into the road's wheel-cut banks. Like fine, pointed metal the branches scratched the sides of Lea's car. Against a spitting summer rain that had turned the dunes dank and dark, the girl's yellow jacket up ahead was slick and synthetic, the color of new pencils or school buses. Something about the way she sat squarely on the motorbike's seat was familiar to Lea, the way she held onto the handlebars with such regal and elastic confidence, bouncing along as the damp, rutted sand flew back under her tires in small, uneven spurts.

Yet as quickly as the girl had appeared, the road turned and Lea lost sight of her. She had wanted the girl to turn her head for a moment so she could see if she knew her. But the road slowly leveled onto high, exposed bluff, and, when Lea finally reached the end of it and got out of the car to take her shoes off for her daily walk, the motorbike lay tossed aside in the sand like a sneaker on a mudroom floor, the simple relic of an afterthought.

From where she stood, high on the dunes next to the car, the sea seemed to lift toward her like a tabletop. The sky bore down, holding the great beach and the distant, naked girl standing on it in perfect, yet tenuous, place. The girl faced the sea, too intent to even feel the mist of rain against the curve of her bare back. She dove, and all that Lea could see was a trail made by her sleek head as it skimmed the surface.

But as Lea descended the long flight of steps and got closer to the girl—who was now running from the water—she saw that the girl's round, peasant face was as miraculous and astonished as Susie's baby face had been emerging from the steam and soap of her bath: a slippery, cooing infant that Lea had held with one arm while grabbing a towel with the other years ago in an old apartment bathroom in New York. Certain memories were remnants—that was how she liked to think of them: tiny broken potsherds to be saved and judiciously tagged, small brief hopes, like those inert moments of peace before she was fully awake in the morning and remembered that life was not as it should be and that Susan was dead.

"Close call!" the girl laughed as Lea approached. She slipped her jeans on as she referred, with a subtle, quick look, to an old man with a cane who was making his way toward them along the shore.

"Ahoy!" the old man yelled as if he were truly at sea and had spotted a ship.

"Ahoy!" the girl yelled back, amused. She zipped up her jeans and bent for her top.

But what a wonder it was to be so graphically reminded of Susan's growing up, those days when she'd stretched—however imperfectly—toward something more adult, her face as she ran into the house from the beach with that vibrant and impatient flush. Time, someone once said, even gives poetry to the scars of battle, and she was grateful for that. But this girl on the beach looked familiar in her own right. Perhaps she'd been in Susan's high school class.

"Be careful swimming without a lifeguard," Lea said.

The girl turned her head and refused to make eye contact, and there it was all over again: the reason they'd referred to Susan as Her Majesty: her habit of turning people off with remote, monarchial assurance if anyone should contradict—or even dare suggest.

"Really," said Lea, "it's dangerous out here. I mean it."

"It's not my turn to drown," the girl said with a dart of wit.

The old man heard the girl's comment. He was now that close.

"I've seen a lot of people die out of turn in my time," he said.

His eyes watered from the wind but gleamed with assurance like the eyes of the elderly always do when presenting irrevocable fact. Yet one could see from this look—if one took the time—that he'd been young once, too, that it had not been so simple giving it all up.

"I've never seen anyone walk with a cane in sand," Lea said.

"It's the idea of it that helps," the old man answered, "not the cane itself."

He waved goodbye with his free hand as he walked off.

"Were you a friend of Susan's?" Lea asked the girl who was now bending to pick up her yellow jacket. "You look so familiar."

"—Susan?"

The girl was quickly alert.

"Susan Ryder. She was my daughter."

"No . . . no," the girl said, suddenly embarrassed. "I didn't even know her."

But she knows *about* Susan, Lea thought. Even people I've never met know, and she flushed.

The girl was clearly anxious to be gone, but Lea wanted her to stop and converse, say something. Just a word or two. A smile or knowing nod would have been enough to erase the sense of ineptitude that Lea suddenly felt, but the girl retreated, scampering up the dune's long line of weathered steps.

"I did it again," she said to a shell with a bore hole that she'd absentmindedly picked up. "I put my foot in it."

The tide washed across the sand in great curving arcs as she walked. The rain gathered and fell, drop by drop, against her face from the plastic visor of her cap. She'd nodded in agreement when the old man had said it's the idea of it that helps, not the cane itself, but she hadn't really understood, hadn't particularly wanted to think about it.

A mile down the beach, the old jetty's tumbled granite boulders, overgrown with moss and mussels, cut across her path, and she decided to head back to the car. A lone gull passed above screeching in displeasure.

"What did you expect?" she asked the irritated gull as he careened out of sight, "A garbage dump with wonderful, rotting scraps?"

The girl had reminded her of Susan, imperious and rejecting and quick. Yet when she thought of the girl's sudden desire to be rid of her, she felt vaguely frightened. It was as if the girl had sensed something that ought to be curtailed, something that Lea herself could not see clearly enough to even begin to correct.

But as she drove home the road began to absorb her pain with a certain still confidence the way sand absorbs heat or moisture. The turnings gave her a sense of safety as, after each turn, the road became a small inclusive place unto itself.

"Enough is enough," she said out loud. "No more!" she said, swearing not to think about the girl. "Poof! She's gone!" and she wiped the condensation on the windshield off in wide, inclusive circles with the heel of her hand.

She turned on the radio, but there was nothing but garbled sound and what might have been an orchestra buried in static. The soft wet sand gave under the tires. The body of the car swung gently as she turned the steering wheel first to the right, easing around one bend, then to the left, easing around the next. She could not see the motorbike's treads on the road in front of her, nor did she hear anything but her own car, the satisfying sound of the motor and the purring of the wipers, that sweet, almost sentimental knock against the glass. It was just that Susan had been the swimming girl's age once. And sometimes that was all it took.

The girl lifted her eyes to the oncoming car and for one strange, elastic moment, as the impact tore against her, her head seemed to rebound off her neck. In a burst of flame the motorbike ricocheted off the front of Lea's car, its crushed gas tank burst apart, and Lea saw the girl hurled into the sky like an acrobat. The sky received and caught her. Held her, it seemed, a rani she became, a princess in remote lethargy dozing on a palanquin of air, a pillowed couch. Her head turned slowly and deliberately as if to stretch or yawn or look about, as if to summon refreshment, rose water, sugared cakes, perhaps. She's like a drunken pasha, Lea thought, in a lovely jacket of gleaming, saffron silk. Fire rained. Sparks fell. One glowing bolus of flame hung menacing and dark, then dropped like an object of war, a clench of smoldering metal streaming sooty ribbons of black smoke. The girl hit the road, limp and light and inanimate.

Lea turned to look through the fogged rear windows for help, but as she got out of the car there was only the motionless girl twisted on the road amidst a scattered assortment of sooty metal, the brief burning into memory of a blackened tailpipe that became—at once and forever in Lea's memory—a charred question mark.

"I just didn't see you," Lea said. "Why did you get off your bike? What were you doing? Why did you stop?"

The girl grimaced and a glistening trickle of black-red blood appeared from her mouth like a small animal and slid across her lower lip.

"Listen," Lea said in sudden fear, "don't move. Someone will be here any minute, I'm sure of it."

But why won't she look at me? Lea thought. Is she angry? Is that it?

"You can count on me. I promise you," Lea said. "I promise I won't leave you until help comes. Not even for an instant."

A cord of blood made its way down the girl's chin and headed for her neck.

"I used to tell my daughter stories," Lea said in desperation. "It always seemed to help."

She took a deep, anxious breath. There was nothing to be done but start.

"I'd tell her how the warblers, the Tennessees and Nashvilles and Cape Mays, were flitting through the trees and scrub, or how the moon was glowing over the hogbacks as it pulled the neap tide further and further in towards itself. I'd explain how grass grew better under locusts than any other kind of tree because of the nitrogen their roots give off, but locusts are fragile, I'd tell her, and storms can easily crack them apart, that's why Daddy trims them down when they grow too close to the house."

My God, what else?

"Storms bring the moles out. They dig under the lawn and make tunnels and nests. They search for grubs when they do that. When you wake up in the morning and come down for breakfast, darling, when you walk across the lawn in your little bare feet, the grass will feel like walking on grandma's old mattress."

The words dissolved around her. Threads in the mist.

"Sweetheart? Did you hear me?" she asked. "Remember the winter we went to Florida?—Remember that? Remember the raccoon that climbed down the chimney into the house . . . ? Oh surely, darling, surely you remember that?"

"Yes, Mommy . . . ," the child said. "I remember that."

Thank God she's talking again, Lea thought.

"We could tell where he'd been from his footprints. Remember?" Lea asked.

"They were all over the place," the child said. "There was soot everywhere—all over the beds and sofa, all over the house! He slept in our beds! Remember, Mommy? He slept in our beds and left footprints all over the house. How did he get out, Mommy? Tell how he got out!"

How Lea loved these moments of forgiveness. Her heart reached out to her little girl as she tried to think what they'd done to get the raccoon out.

"I don't know, sweetheart," for her mind went momentarily blank. "I can't remember that part."

She looked down at her daughter and tried to remember how they'd gotten the raccoon out. She looked at the face, the porcelain eyes that stared at nothing at all, the strange slack curve of the cheek and jaw, and saw that the still gray face, the pinpoint pupils like dots at the end of a page, the blond hair cropped short were not Susan's at all. They belonged to someone else. How strange, she thought, trying to remember just who the girl was and why they were both there.

"So much gets lost," she said with confusion. "So much

gets erased. I was going to copy down all those stories I used to tell her, the clever little things she said in response, but I never did. I could have caught her voice on tape. My parents gave us a tape recorder for that very purpose, but I wouldn't take the time, because I never had enough time. Perhaps she hated me for that."

In the far distance a shaft of flat sun caught a cluster of gulls circling like a small cloud of gnats. Focusing like a daydreamer on this small, dissipating cloud seemed to help. For a moment she remembered being in labor, focusing on a series of infinitesimal spots on a delivery room wall.

"Maybe I was just too young to be a mother. I thought too much about myself. But I should have taped your voice. I should have done that. I should have saved your childhood not just for you, darling, but for all of us."

It was that hour of the day—she could see it now, the angle of that one shaft of sun told it. The hour of the day when everything becomes a heavier commodity. Time weighs and nothing's sold for simply cost.

"But I wasn't such a bad mother. . . . Was I?"

Susie's eyes said it all. She was angry again.

"Darling, why must you always put me through this?" Lea asked.

The Visiting Room

Even in his prison jumpsuit, General Cerjak could have been nothing but a general.

"Yes," he said across the small green painted table, "I tell from the face. With the high forehead, the ears wide apart, you are clever. Brain power." For one still moment, his glasses caught the flat, barred light from the window.

"Phrenology," I said. "That's what we call it."

He shifted with impatience in his chair, and my own reflection suddenly appeared twice, one tiny, rounded image in each lens of his thick glasses. Yet I only recognized these images—so reduced in size and minute in detail—as myself because it could have been no one else.

"This incarceration is—of course—political," he said.

I looked at his taciturn face and prison haircut, his newly shaved chin with one thin red razor scratch.

"Six hundred years and the battle continues. This is what you have done," he said. "You and your NATO."

"Of course others don't see it that way," I said, suddenly discomfited at stating the obvious.

He half-rose, supported by his hands on the table, and his face inclined toward me.

"The Mother of God has decreed," he said with displeasure.

I glanced instinctively at the guard standing with legs splayed into waiting stance by the locked metal door, but he stood as in a trance, glazed eyes, turned in our direction, showing no interest.

"We build a church on Kosovo," the general said, his face precipitously close to my own. "Not with marble floors we build. We build with silk. We build with scarlet!"

The word *scarlet* came toward me like a small angry missile. I had a sudden desire to lean back with an assured motion as I would have in the comfortable and protective armchair of my office. But the flimsy little prison chair prevented it.

"As for this trial," he said, "you can write it in your newspaper, Mr. Hammond: Only the victors try the vanquished."

He sat back down as if he knew exactly what his own chair required and what he could expect from it.

With studied calm, I took a pack of cigarettes out of my pocket and rapped it against the side of my hand so that one filtered cigarette reluctantly slid part-way out.

"Bad for the lungs," he said, as I held out the pack, so I placed the cigarettes back in my pocket.

I lifted the lid of my briefcase and took out two pads of paper and two pens—enough for us both—then lowered the top and snapped it shut.

"I understand your lawyers are using the Geneva Convention's definition of genocide in your defense," I said. "It's the toughest charge to prove. The court's never once been able to show that killings have been systematic and widespread on the basis of anything national, religious, or ethnic."

He looked at me with barely veiled contempt.

"You are young at this, are you not?" he asked.

"I'm qualified," I said.

"I am no journalist, but over the years I have interrogated

many men. Interrogation takes a certain talent. I could show you how to do it."

The metal frames of his glasses flashed a sudden star of light which seemed to mock, "You speak of war, Mr. Hammond, as if it were a game that comes with little tin soldiers wrapped in a box."

"I'm talking about military law, General."

"Yet would you not say that war, by its very nature, is outside the meaning of laws? Even outside the language we have to explain it?"

"It seems to me they'll convict you on the spot if you come up with that kind of thing in court."

"In war there is no such thing as a weighted—we will say, measured—response. That is the face of truth. You tell me that you are a journalist, Mr. Hammond. Is truth not what you want?"

"There have to be rules of conduct in any war, General. Like it or not, it's as simple as that."

"You would do well to become familiar with America's second war of aggression against the Indochinese," he said. "Where is Mr. Calley now? And the four soldiers who captured the Asian girl and took her into the jungle? How long did your country keep these men in jail? And where are their superiors who stayed quiet?"

Her name was Alicia and she was clearly embarrassed. Another girl from town, who had come to the party with Jimmy Neal, had fixed the two of us up. But Alicia was the kind of girl who didn't know how to converse or even make small talk. Maybe she'd never been on a date before. And she was the kind of girl who apologizes for everything that happens to her because she thinks it's her own fault. But what I noticed most of all was that she had a front tooth with a chip out of it. It was that chipped tooth, more than anything else, that reminded me she was different than the girls on campus; any girl I knew would have had the money and good sense to get it capped.

I worked my way over to the wet bar to get us both beers, and, as I pushed my way back through the crowd to bring it to her, I saw her sitting on the edge of the couch and waiting for me like someone in a dentist's office when they're too nervous to pick up a magazine to distract themselves. They might sit there for hours and never once go up to the little window and question the receptionist.

"Have you never killed a man, Mr. Hammond?"

That's what he asked me, as if the interview were not about him at all. I should have answered him plainly and easily—conversationally. But I didn't. Instead I pretended to ignore him and said, "I understand your lawyers are going to demonstrate a breakdown in field communications between you and your troops for the crimes against humanity and war crimes charges. But the rape accusations may be a problem. The prosecution is bound to argue that your presence at the school proves you sanctioned them."

"They have no witnesses to any sanctioning, Mr. Hammond."

"Two of the women were virgins at the time of the rapes, one was eight months pregnant, and one was a child only ten years old. You can be sure they'll make the most of that."

"You are not a soldier, Mr. Hammond. Let me ask you—for example—this: Have you never acted aggressively toward a party of the opposite sex?"

He looked straight at me with those hard blue eyes behind

those thick glasses of his, and his look never wavered. Not once. What he saw or did not see I couldn't tell. Yet with the sweet taste of discovery that may have been feigned—or may have been real—he asked, "Have you never raped, Mr. Hammond?"

But, again, I held on and ignored the question, though it should have been clear to me by now that this wasn't the most effective tactic.

"It sounds as if you're going to go against the advice of counsel," I said. "You seem to be professing guilt."

"Not at all," he answered. "Not at all," and he flashed a hardly benign smile. For a moment he sounded almost jovial. "On the contrary. It is you who are professing guilt."

He stood up and extended his hand and I followed suit. Then with one last demonstration of power he established the interview schedule.

"We will begin tomorrow at ten o'clock." Then he added, "We will do fine, you and myself."

What I had thought of as a coup—landing the seven interviews that the general had agreed to do with the paper—now seemed like some small battered thing, something impotent and nude, dismissively tossed onto the green painted table between us.

Yet he was so beautifully certain in all that he said and did. I still envy him for that.

⁓

Jimmy Neal—on the other hand—my buddy who fixed me up with Alicia, wasn't certain about anything. He looked like the rock of Gibraltar when he was sober: decisive, steady smile and strong jaw, black wavy hair on top, but he wasn't. As soon as you agreed to do one thing, he wanted to do something else. His date had disappeared so he latched onto Alicia sitting on the couch. His right hand swooped through the air like an airplane, and his fists gently trembled the way a plane does when it takes off. He was talking about aerodynamics again, his favorite subject.

But Deirdre Dixon was my true interest. She'd stood me up when we were freshmen, and it still burned me when I saw her. I'd tell myself she was just a slut, but the truth of it was I still wanted to go out with her. And there she was—red hair and all—making out and slow dancing at the same time with Mick Henshaw over in one corner.

Sure, I'd had too much to drink, but nobody else was feeling any pain either, guys who I really loved in those years, who'd stick up for you no matter what, never let you down kind of thing, but who at some of those parties were incommunicado. Once I'd gone over my limit I didn't care about anything much. I just wanted to go home and lie down flat, because, to tell you the truth, drinking has always made me sick.

Maybe that's just my excuse for everything that happened next, because I was certainly sober enough to remember the major part of it.

Yet sometimes when I try to think of her, a melting light seems to step into my mind, and she begins to vanish. That's when I reach out into the hemisphere and grab onto her floating body with both my hands and bring her back. Some say remembering is the most courageous act of all. And this is why I do it: because there are no other acts of bravery or daring, no acts of contrition, in my past.

The room and its metal door, in front of which stood the guard, were painted the exact institutional green of the table.

"Do you have a family?" I asked.

"So it is. We are not now on war crimes. We are on the human interest story."

"I suppose you could put it like that."

"My wife's name is Trahina. We have always been loyal to each other. Three sons and two daughters. And you?"

"I'm alone at the moment. No sons, no daughters."

He made a sympathetic sound and continued, "They broke open my front door in Trobloko at two in the morning. They bound my children and my wife with tape and locked them in the closets. The youngest dropped her doll onto the floor, Miska—she called this baby of hers. A soldier's boot crushed the belly of it. I have my child's scream, now, always in my head. My wife and children in the dark closets bound with hands behind their backs. They took my briefcase and computer and floppy disks. All this while a NATO helicopter hovered over the house. I myself was driven to Sarajevo and put on a plane to The Hague, then driven to this prison. All in my pajamas. The pilot gave me an overcoat and a pair of boots. As you can see," he said sarcastically, "in this beautiful and historic prison, I have no need for my own clothes. I have food and water, exercise, and my own private toilet."

He watched me jotting down details, the duct tape and doll, the loaned boots and coat, the theft of his computer and floppy disks. Then he said, "The guards say from the towers you see a tremendous beautiful beach with many sunbathers. Windsurfers with brightly colored sails flying like birds across the water. Women without bathing tops. Is this so? I myself do not believe it, but they say it is true."

"Different than Trobloko," I said.

"A deep ancestry Trobloko has. Deep as the eye of God. A town many centuries old in the curve of a valley. A lake reflecting the heavens and always filled with trout. I tell my wife they bite her toes and she laughs." His face softened as he thought of it. "Many trout suspended and still when one looks down through the surface of the water."

This listening, then recounting, of others' lives was what I did best. But what he said next brought me up short.

"You see, Mr. Hammond, I have left you alone. I have not inquired into—what shall we call it?—your own personal problems. I have left the wall up. The sign says do not enter and I have not trespassed."

Yet certain motivations leave an imprint. Trace around their shapes and cut them out and their borders will exactly fit, though to some it might seem they're not the same at all.

↳

But I just wanted to forget Alicia—Deirdre Dixon, too, for that matter—and go home. I walked over to her and Jimmy Neal sitting on the couch and said her name to myself, but not to her at all. I guess because I'd had too much to drink. Maybe I was just trying to remember it.

"Alicia," I said. "Alicia."

Jimmy Neal said something about driving me home. I couldn't afford a car in those days; I had to pay for everything myself. Case Stanton said he wanted to go along to pick up more beer. Case could get pretty rough when he was drunk, but I wasn't thinking about that then, and anyway, who in those situations ever prepares for the worst?

The four of us got into the car, me and Jimmy Neal in the front, Case and the girl, Alicia, in the back, and that's when Whitey Swinbeck, who had white blond hair and a face that was always too red to go with it, staggered up to the car and said he wanted to go with us, and if we had a girl all the better, and Case said good thing we had a girl, and he knew what girls were for. So including Whitey Swinbeck, who piled in the back with Case and the girl, that made five of us. Whitey Swinbeck teaches history now at some junior college out west. I got invited to his daughter's wedding in California last winter, but I couldn't make it. I was seeing a woman at the paper who had two little boys and we'd planned to take them on a two-week vacation to Barbados.

General Cerjak had drawn a series of little hedged mazes one after the other in perfect perspective on his pad of paper.

"Tell me about the 28th of April," I said.

Someone in the prison must have turned on a radio, because I heard a guitar and a voice like John Denver's singing through the walls. The guard's expressionless Dutch eyes stared toward the window. From where I sat, he stared into a gray, barred rectangle.

"That famous day in Provsky," the general said, "is not interesting. I have read the Geneva Convention and been informed. Violations of the laws or customs of wars in the former Yugoslavia. The obligations of international law. The responsibility of superiors for the acts of their subordinates. But I do not agree with this. It is those who commit the crimes who are guilty, not those of us who sit many miles away in an office, and they should be tried in their own country's courts."

"So you don't believe that those who are aware of a crime and do nothing about it are also culpable?"

"Why do they say nothing, Mr. Hammond? Why, when the bell of conscience rings for them do they choose not to listen to it? It is because they know that certain unpleasant acts—most especially in war—are natural. Hate is like a tree with many green leaves and deep roots. The leaves die and it is winter. Snow falls and all is peaceful. But then rain clouds come and feed the tree and it bears fruit."

I can't remember who started in on her first, but somebody in the backseat, probably Case, asked her if she liked to kiss, and she said no, no she didn't, she just wanted to go home, and could we please take her home, and Whitey Swinbeck in the back with them just laughed.

"Knock it off, Case," I said from the front.

"Go ahead," he said. "Stop the car, Jimmy. Dave wants a fight."

"Just forget it, Case," I said, but he didn't hear me. He was too busy with Alicia, who was explaining that we should have turned right two streets back, because her house was on one of those streets that came up from the river.

"Yea, yea . . . ," Jimmy Neal said. "Why the hell you want to go home? Don't you like us? What you think, Case, should we take her on home?"

"Please," she said.

"I'm not your type?" Case asked.

Then she said something about liking everyone and not wanting to have any feelings hurt.

"That was a definite no, Case," I said from the front seat with my eyes closed and my head back. "She's not your type and you know it."

"I just want to go home," Alicia said.

"Shut up, bitch!" Case said, and Alicia didn't say anything else.

They laughed and carried on, handing an open beer around, and singing some song about a girl named Lulu. Not until we pulled into the lot of the convenience store did Alicia say that if we didn't mind waiting could she please get out to go to the ladies' room.

"Sure, sure," Jimmy Neal said.

Whitey Swinbeck got out of the car and Alicia started to follow when Case grabbed onto her arm and held it tight.

"Hold on, bitch," he said.

"Hell, Case," I said, "why talk to her like that?"

"What's the matter with you, Dave? You got a burr up your ass?"

She tried to pull free from Case's grip.

"That hurts!" she said.

"Hell, Stanton, you want her to have an accident?" Jimmy Neal asked.

"She isn't going anywhere," Case said.

We turned into Old Hollow Road where it passes the mill. The mill was closed and dark except for a few muddy-looking, yellow pools of light in the parking lot.

"Go down the fire road behind Nealey's," Case said. "They've got a night watchman here."

Alicia began to beg, "Please don't . . . please . . . " and that kind of thing in a strange, whimpery voice.

I had my eyes closed and my head back, trying not to throw up. We were on unpaved road, and the way Jimmy Neal was driving didn't help. I'd open up my eyes and there would be those shreds of decaying fabric from the ceiling hanging down and vibrating with the rhythm of the car, and I could hear Case say, "Come on, honey, you know you like that. Don't lie to Case, baby, you know you love me doing that."

"The last thing I need is to get stuck on some dirt road," Jimmy Neal said. "I'm pulling over." He stopped the car and turned the headlights off.

There was trash like fast-food wrappers and bottles and such all over the place, but I just wanted to lie down on the ground on my back, and I didn't much care if I was lying on trash or not.

⁓

"I know about the community of the world, as you call it," the general said, "the United States of America. I am, as you say, a history buff. I know it better than you. For example, there was General Sherman. He is famous for the burning of civilian dwellings. He wrote a letter to the mayor of a city called Atlanta. But never mind what General Sherman says. You ask for a story. The truth of war, yes?"

"April 28th," I said.

"Twenty-eight April we came into Provsky, two battalions, in order to secure the populace from which we know there were many Muslim dissidents. Houses with ammunition, et cetera. Not one of them could we trust. They were too sure of how they thought it was. They thought to stay in their homes like little weasels in winter and then sneak out and kill us as we passed. The rail yard was the most difficult area. We could not secure these houses. The women and children were absolute sure of themselves, taunting as we passed in the trucks or patrolling on foot. I myself was hit by a rock thrown by a child not more than eight years old. I gave the order in the afternoon of 28 April to round them up. Every house between Provsky Square and the train depot. What was I to do? Put them to bed for the night and feed them with fairy tales and prayers? In the morning send them back to their houses so they would be happy and fire more guns and throw rocks at us? They were taken to the school—which was empty at the time—and shot. Not all. To be exact twenty-three male prisoners were kept alive. They were sent north."

"And the rapes?"

"Some were raped."

"Did you, in any way, participate?"

"I ordered the shootings and prisoner transports, yes. The rapes I did not."

"Did you see any of the rapes take place?"

"I did not."

"Then how do you know they happened?"

"You sound like a lawyer, Mr. Hammond, but I forgive you for that."

I lay on the ground and looked up through the trees, and everything was spinning like when you're a kid and you make yourself dizzy by turning around and around as fast as your body will go until you finally fall down into a crumpled heap on the ground.

But the stars above didn't move; they held completely still. I wondered how they could stay so perfectly quiet, yet watchful and alert. It seemed to me I was on top of the earth and the earth was a mountain with trees and woods and ground sloping down on every side away from it. But the minute I tried to sit up the nausea and dizziness came rushing back.

They must have moved off into the woods, because all I remember hearing was a rustling like animals make in the dark when they're searching for things to build a nest. I don't know what animals do in the woods at night. Hunt for food, I guess. But I'll never forget those stars and how they hung there all by themselves. They just about had me in their pocket.

"All this time," said the general, "you are begging for confession from me. You want me on my knees before God's throne. Just as the court will beg for some contrite thing—no matter how small—to pass from my lips."

"I simply want your story," I said. "Nothing more, nothing less."

The general raised a hand as if to demand silence, but for the moment, I wasn't going to let him have it.

"As far as I'm concerned," I said, "a man's confessions are private."

"You in America think a man is either good or evil, that he cannot be both, but listen and I will tell you how the Lord God made man."

As he spoke his cloak of authority assumed a slightly different—more ecclesiastical—color, and I saw something that I hadn't seen before.

"I never understood why you agreed to these interviews," I said.

But he wasn't listening. If he had been, I might have told him that he was exercising—because he found joy in it—his most proficient talents.

"The light was clear and bright," he said. "Like water it was. The dark deeper than the longest night. They were far apart this dark and light. So the Lord God pushed back the sleeve of his garment, and with his thumb, dipped into the dark, then into the light. Then with this thumb that had been dipped in both, onto the world he made a mark."

He pressed an invisible smudge onto the table with his thumb in order to demonstrate man's birth.

And I saw that he'd taken his glasses off. His eyes, freed from their thickness of protective glass, were moist and deep, and weightless.

"Mr. Hammond, you wish to pretend that no one but yourself can see your own dark. You shelter it. You almost nurture it. There is nothing easier for the eye than a man in hiding. He always stands out."

His hands delicately cradled his glasses, a fragile wire-and-glass prosthesis. "When I was a boy in my village," he said, "I would lie on my belly in the sun and watch the small lizards. Dark like tar, they were under the leaves. Then gray the color of mortar as they ran up the walls."

I must have fallen asleep, because when I finally stood up, the three of them were staggering and laughing around the car, but I didn't see Alicia anywhere. Then I was suddenly sick. I turned and heaved and everything came up.

"You go get her and take her home," Whitey Swinbeck said to me. "She's no good to anyone now."

And for the first time I thought about her actually being hurt. I knew these guys, they were friends of mine, but when Whitey said that I, honest to God, thought for a moment that she was dead and I didn't understand it.

"We shouldn't have left her lying there," Jimmy Neal said. "Suppose she can't walk?"

"We were supposed to be taking her home," I said.

"Shut up, Dave," Case said. "You can do what you want, but I'm getting out of here."

"As far as I'm concerned, this never happened," said Whitey Swinbeck.

"Come on, Dave. You want to be left holding the bag?" Jimmy Neal asked.

"Get in the car," Case said.

I got in the front with Jimmy Neal behind the wheel and the four of us started back.

"See what you missed, Davy, see what you missed?" Case

dangled something that looked like women's underwear in front of my face.

"We ought to go back and get her and have Dave take her home," Jimmy Neal said. "I never should have gone along with this."

"But you did, Jimmy boy, you did. Because you wanted some," Case said.

General Cerjak turned to the guard standing by the door. "Water," he said.

The guard rang a button on the wall, and another guard's head showed through the door's small barred window.

"Water," the first guard said, and the other's head disappeared.

The skin under the general's eyes and around his mouth reminded me of the tired creases of an old man's shirt.

"I should have thought of the water myself," I said, apologetic.

"They have women who say they heard me sanction their defilement. My lawyers tell me this. These women lie. But what is so unusual about that? People lie all the time. Or they remain quiet. Silence and lies are the same thing. Yet always one pays for not speaking out. If one has no voice, what is he? Would you say he is alive or dead? Or perhaps a combination of the two? A living corpse?"

"There's always the appeal process."

"The love of one's own people is one of God's laws, Mr. Hammond. Whatever my future is to be, God has chosen it with his own hand."

A guard's head reappeared at the window in the door. The guard inside opened the door and received two metal cups of water. The door closed with a sound of heavy, but final, restraint and the guard placed the two metal cups on the small, green painted table.

"It may be that I will never touch the skin of my wife again or see the eyes of my children when I bring them their gifts. I will live in this prison forever in a flat gray country that has passion for nothing but order."

His sad eyes looked at me.

"But you, Mr. Hammond, what will you—and all the rest—ask on appeal? The rescinding of one charge of genocide, three charges of crimes against humanity, and four charges of war crimes? Have you been accused of shelling and sniping to kill, maim, wound, and otherwise terrorize civilian inhabitants? Of overseeing forced relocations and the destruction of property belonging to Muslims?"

I suddenly wanted to give him an answer. I could almost have said the words.

He raised his cup of water carefully with both hands and held it high. For a moment his hands seemed to disappear, and I saw only the metal cup suspended above us.

"Mother of God," he said, "take please our gifts. Make all holy and honorable until the goodness of God is fulfilled. Remember to us this day, Holy Mother, the sacred place of water."

His hands gently lowered as if the cup were full to the brim and he was fearful of spilling a drop. Only when the cup was back on the table and he had taken a drink of it, only then did he turn and look at the guard. Yet the guard still stared out the small barred window. Perhaps he'd learned that slight form of concealed sleep so common to guards. Perhaps he saw something there beyond the bars. Or perhaps the gray mist and bars were simply a backdrop to some thought or memory I could not have guessed at.

The general's gaze followed the guard's as if it were a beam. And mine followed the general's. For a moment no longer than the interval between two thoughts, the three of us stared at the small barred receding rectangle. Then the general moved his torso to get up and take his leave. His feet shifted, and his chair creaked, and the guard's blank gaze turned toward the two of us.

The Secret Life of Objects

Walking into their bedroom, I heard a restive sound as if all the contents of the room had shifted slightly and then leaned forward to see which one of us had come back. The drapes were drawn, blocking out the street of ailing elms and dilapidated row houses, muffling in dark the wallpaper and the pictures against it.

Yet when I turned the lamp on, I saw that the room held twice the furniture I remembered and that it lay under a blanket of detritus which, as I stood there listening, seemed to let out a sharp, aggrieved breath like an old man suddenly struck by a heavy pain in his chest. Or an old woman, unsteady with walker, looking down with a gasp to find her husband dead on the worn bedroom carpet, then crumpling herself, leaving her cracked black purse, which she carried even to bed, abandoned beside her.

The ambulance crew had taken the two of them away without touching the purse, and I remembered that one of the things I'd come for was my mother's cameo brooch of the goddess Minerva. It had been a wedding gift from my father.

So much had disappeared into the hole of their death, I suddenly didn't want anything else to be lost, but in sitting on the floor and spreading the contents of the purse out on the carpet, I saw that the cameo wasn't there. There's no light switch in a purse, no bulb on its ceiling as there is in a closet. And nobody likes to go into the dark alone. But I saw that there was nothing left inside. Only the lining of worn black fabric made slick by an accumulation of wear and dirt.

Everything had fallen out onto the carpet: A pair of my father's glasses with a missing lens. A gently bent cigarette. A golf tee caught in the spidery filaments of a hair net. The metal cap from a shattered Christmas ornament. A thumbtack. A rubber pessary. Some shreds of tobacco. A wind-up key for who knows what, perhaps a mechanical toy or clock. A filigree costume jewelry earring in poor imitation of lace. Three bobby pins. A yellowed recipe from the newspaper for Almond Velvet folded several times over into the size of a postage stamp. A Hershey Kiss melted into its little paper tag and thin foil wrap. Several small and large paper clips. A matchbox with a yellow dragon breathing a jagged curl of fire out of its mouth. A small six-pointed metal object that I recognized as a jack. An acorn painted with primitive mouth and eyes by a schoolchild. A spool of beige silk thread. A rigor-mortised sparrow with curling feet and eyes clamped shut. Half a Pink Pearl eraser. A Trenton Rotary Club tie clip. A green marble. A gauge to measure tire pressure. A garter belt. A peppermint turned to white dust in its twisted cellophane wrapper. A hospital identification bracelet on which was typed my mother's full name and social security number: Brenda Phyllis Johnson 487-40-7855. A thick blue rubber band similar to those that hold bunches of broccoli tightly together in the supermarket. And a souvenir Atlantic City key ring with a seahorse encased in Plexiglas. Soon I had each thing separate on the floor and remembered in my mind. Yet these objects seem strangely malevolent to me when I think about them. Though perhaps it's unfair to accuse these few simple things, for nothing knows better, nothing is more sympathetic to the need to feel deeply and be remembered than an object. Nothing is more aware of the need to separate, the desire to wall off, or has a greater need to advance itself.

With its scorched shade, a limp necktie and brassiere draped over it, the lamp saw my face all lit, remembered me in my child's nightgown knocking not once or twice in fright but a dozen or so times on the door to wake my parents up after my body had been erased by the dark. Taken into their bed, I became as small as a dot. Then conversely, enlarged beyond the bounds of earth before slowly dissipating in the sound of their sleeping breath, the rush of flying geese and dry leaves scraping across frozen water that always came from the feather pillows, the shadow of a hand flinging the grain for the geese across the hard-packed earth that swept across my sleeping form and always drew me back.

Now as I sat on the same bed and held a baby picture of my father staring bright and amazed at the camera, I remembered that he had never, in his long and uneventful life, traveled outside his own country, never dated anyone but my mother. He'd had dreams of becoming an economist but was never more than an accountant. His only love was what he called books of importance, the same books he was always giving my mother in the vain hope that she'd read even just one of them. A man whose senility, in later life, gnawed at his virtues and turned him into his worst self.

In her own photograph my mother stands before a bower of trees, the cotton of her white dress luminous substance against the dusk, her face obliterated by shadow. Only a point of silver nose hangs like a coin under her wide-brimmed hat. This picture, taken years before the next, in which both of them stand with their eldest in front of the house before my birth.

How I dislike that cradle over the abyss, the dark that frames our lives with the knowledge that one's family once lived perfectly well without us. My father glares at the camera, wanting it over. My mother looks bereft. Joshua, who I always associate with the ham radio left in the attic, stands beside my sister April who left a cupboard full of dolls from foreign countries when she went off to college. And Janine who was bookish and sent me a slipcased copy of *A Shropshire Lad* when I was fifteen, illustrated with delicate wood engravings in the style of Thomas Hart Benton. *O see how thick the goldcup flowers are lying in field and lane, with dandelions to tell the hours that never are told again.* It gives one the urge to repeat such things if only for a moment of poetic pleasure. Joshua, April, and Janine all wishing with pained expressions that they were somewhere else. Which they are now. So scattered with families of their own they hardly seemed to care when I called to break the news and said I was going back to close up the house. Perhaps they just didn't know what to say because so much time had passed.

And the black telephone on my mother's bedside table, the memory of its strident ringing and the suspense of who might be calling next. Those calls my aging mother made in secret so as not to be damned by my increasingly cantankerous father for her one or two remaining friendships. The same phone on which a neighbor had called for an ambulance after breaking out a pane and climbing through the kitchen window.

Joyce's *Dubliners* on my father's bedside stand. The marked passages that seemed to dispute the curmudgeon he so often was, the apex of a folded corner pointing the way to lines encased in his unmistakable penciled brackets: *But real adventures, I reflected, do not happen to people who remain at home: they must be sought abroad.* And: *Her name was like a summons to all my foolish blood. But my body was like a harp and her words and gestures were like fingers running upon the wires.* Lines that must have referred to my mother.

A carton of adult-sized disposable diapers. Stacks of *Ladies Home Journal*s and *National Geographic*s. Costume jewelry necklaces and limp socks draped over the corner of a mirror along with yards of clear plastic tubing dangling from a disposable oxygen mask. Certain objects tell certain stories to each other. They are like collaborators or small children whispering back and forth in the dark, causing our childhoods and adulthoods, our waking life and dreams, to intersect.

In another photograph the three of us, my mother and father and myself, stand ankle-deep in dirty slush in front of a battered car. Beyond the car a portion of familiar white painted spindled railing binds a corner of the front porch.

My mother and father and myself all stand in front of the unpleasant car, which I assume, because we're holding gifts, we were about to get into to make our annual Christmas visits. Dressed in ill-fitting coats and tremendous long scarves, ragged mittens and woolen caps, the three of us stand cold and uncomfortable. A striped wool cap is pulled down over my ears and forehead, its baseball-sized pom-pom about to fall off. My nervous mother grabs a leash attached to the collar of an equally nervous wrinkle-faced pug, whose name was Boots. He stands by my booted feet with his tongue hanging out, one disagreeable tooth escaped outside his mouth. It was the last picture ever taken of the three of us. My mother had once miscarried after visiting a photography studio so my father was convinced that photography was bad luck. Anything that multiplies the image of man can't be trusted, he'd say. That includes mirrors and copulation and photographs. Yet in spite of its dour aspect, this newly created photograph seemed more important to me than anything else.

More important, for example, than my great grandmother's pearl ring, which I had worn for years on my right third finger. Though in the normal hierarchy of things, the ring would certainly be worth more than a dour, yellowed photograph. The photograph worth more than the slippers repaired with masking tape, or the knit hat whose replaced elastic, winding through the crocheted brim to tighten it, read *Jockey . . . Jockey . . . Jockey . . .* just as it once had on a pair of my father's discarded undershorts. Yet, when I think about it, none of these things can truly be said to be more indicative than the dead fly on the windowsill or the curled gray hair imprisoned within the bristles of a brush. Nothing has more immediate credence than the sticky, artless fingerprints left on a bedside water glass.

My mother had stood with her walker in front of the mirror and stretched a yellow-toothed smile, rolled her lips together and folded a Kleenex to blot. Her free hand lifted to her hair and hesitated as if only just discovering that it was no longer sleek and black. Her bereaved gaze in the mirror traveled beyond herself to the cowbell hanging from the closet doorknob by its leather strap; there her gaze stopped. Suddenly, as I watch, she ceases to exist in the glass.

Once, then twice, the bell clanged as I lifted it. For the moment that I stood and held it, the clapper with its bell attached to the darkly worn leather strap was the still, heavy center of my world. All else moved into the distance in ever-widening orbits like multiple planets in a child's science book. But I still needed hard evidence. Objects are pure in their own experience, pure in themselves. Yet so distorted by our own endless travails that no one should begrudge them their day in court.

The first dresser drawer pulled open with a deeply resistant groan but contained only handkerchiefs wadded into stained balls and hosiery tied into dust-brown knots. The next drawer was a jumble of stale-smelling slips, lifeless bras, underpants bound at the waist and legs with rippled, stretched-out elastic. All exhaled that particular odor of skin and unwashed hair, talcum powder and Evening in Paris cologne that had been my aging mother. But the third contained the nightgowns I was looking for. Each faded pink bodice was stained with faint, indelible rust.

So one remembers whether one wants to or not. Because whether we like it or not, every object remembers us. The slips and bras, pants and nightgowns, the recipe for Almond Velvet and the lone filigree earring all remembered an old woman picking up one thing and then another, carrying each thing to a new location in the house. Leaving the toothbrushes—to my father's endless and cruel annoyance—in the silverware drawer, his slippers outside in the mailbox, unopened bills and junk mail, multiple coupons for contests, stacked in a pantry cupboard behind the never-used Steuben wineglasses. Just as the golf tee and Trenton Rotary Club tie clip, the bent cigarette and dragon matchbox, remembered my father though they were carried in my mother's purse.

Yet I, his own flesh and blood, could not remember his voice or his hands or the way he wore his hair. I could not remember my mother's inflections when she spoke. That certain way she had of looking at me as her words formed. My father's grave bedside story-telling manner.

Rain hit the windshield in slick needle drops. Warehouses and train yards and a whole field of iron barrels, mountains of tires, a chemical factory with palatial rows of glittering lights, dissolved under a sky heavy and black. The moon rose, a bloated orange far in the distance off to my left. The clock on the dashboard read 12:14 A.M. Over four hundred miles to go before I'd be home. The digital numbers slid from one minute to the next, each minute strangely interminable. Impossible to judge when 12:15, then 12:16 would suddenly flash. As if each minute were a small, silent coin that knew—without a doubt—it would pass from one brief owner to the next.

I tried to remember my mother, the way she had laughed or sometimes been admonishing and sharp. That combination of movement and glance and voice, her turn of the head. Her way of quickly walking into the bedroom and surveying its contents as she held up my father's just-ironed shirts to hang them in the closet. The way she stood with her weight on her right foot in her tufted cotton bathrobe, her hip turned slightly out, her dark hair only quickly combed back with her own fingers as she rearranged, with a fork, rashers of bacon sizzling in an iron skillet.

When she'd become old and infirm I'd sat by her chair and asked, "Mother, do you know who I am?"

"Yes, of course, dear," she said. "You're Janine."

"No, Mother. I'm the youngest. I'm Laura. The one born last."

"Laura?" she asked wide-eyed. "Who's Laura?"

"You know me, Mamma. I'm the one that stayed the longest."

I'd forgotten to roll up the car window after the last tollbooth and a spray of rain hit the side of my face then slid under the collar of my blouse. Blurred lights appeared in the far distance. Points of sullen and unknowable recognition.

When I was a child I thought I could see in the pearl on my mother's hand the markings of an unknown face like the man in the moon.

"Perhaps it's you," my mother had said. "Perhaps it's not a man at all, Lowy. Perhaps it's you, the little girl in the moon."

Behind the two hands, one smooth and long and lean wearing the pearl, the other baby fat and pink, the table receded like night except for the circle under the lamp where the dark wood gleamed.

She twisted the cellophane wrapper off a peppermint and placed the round white candy precariously on my fat, little thumb.

"See, Mamma. We're the same," I said.

"Yes, Lowy. We're each other." And the peppermint fell off my thumb onto the table with a tiny, hard tap before rolling to the edge and falling softly onto the carpet.

"Senile!" my father spat out years later as he hung the heavy bell around her neck. He could just as well have been talking about himself.

"No, Daddy," I told him on that particular visit, "only stricken in years. Please don't hang that bell on her."

"Have to. Otherwise she'll walk off."

"She's not big enough to make it clang," I said.

The bell on its leather strap had descended over my mother's old head with its curling white hair to hang with its terrible weight against her chest.

"Honey? Janine?" my mother had said. "Can you help me?"

She'd walk through town in her nightgown, clutching her black purse, the cowbell around her neck, her head held high with fragile dignity as she pretended to shop. Grave and delicate and refined, she gazed into store windows, entered the stores and browsed, inspected one thing and then another, had tried to converse, tried to buy things with no money. Once attempted to go to Piscataway on a city bus to visit her long-deceased sister, Margaret. My father would go out looking and usually find her before the police brought her back. Then he'd lead her home with the leather strap. I remembered the dull metallic sound of the clapper as my mother bent down to pick up a feather, my father, perhaps for the moment forgetting that what he led was his wife, yanked hard at the strap.

I remembered the blurred street and overhanging trees, the sudden indefinite and impossible day, my own painful inaction as, fainthearted and bereft, I pretended I hadn't seen them and quickly walked across the street to the opposite sidewalk.

The moon was down, and the rain had stopped, and I was almost home when I realized I'd forgotten to stop by the mortuary to pick up the ashes. I'd only taken a few things from the house: some pieces of costume jewelry, a Droste cocoa tin filled with buttons that I'd used to form into intricate patterns on the flowered living room carpet, and the black purse heavy with contents. I'd completely forgotten about the cameo brooch, but now I suddenly wondered where it was and felt strangely bereft without it. When I was a child I'd hold it in the palm of my hand, and my mother would tell me the story of Minerva, goddess of wisdom, and Arachne, the simple peasant girl. How out of jealousy at Arachne's superior weaving Minerva braided a long strand of yarn and strangled Arachne by winding it around her neck. Then, with repentance, lifted her from the noose and showered a magic liquid over her, transforming Arachne into a spider so that her ability to weave would be forever restored. My mother had leaned toward me to say in a deep conspiratorial whisper: "Don't tell anyone, Lowy, but you're the best."

"Really, Mamma? Really?" I'd asked.

"Yes," she said definitively. "The best."

"Why, Mamma?" I'd asked, wanting proof. "Why am I the best?"

"Because you feel the deepest."

Finally home and exhausted, I crawled into my own bed in my own bedroom and slept. The deep pile of a dark, maroon carpet rose in a forest of disfigured branches and ragged bushes above my head. In front of me a diamond of my own height emitted glittering murky shadows from its planed facets as slick as glass, and I thought, it's trying to tell me something like the flickering lights that extraterrestrials beam from spaceships. Above my head a crescent moon of trimmed fingernail hung precariously on a featherlike branch. I tried to work my way around all this and somehow find a path, but I was blocked by an irregular pyramid of shaved pencil point reclining on its side and shoved against a battered Valium pill, which was slowly being ingested by a great dust mite with loudly cracking jaw and swaying appendages. Hundreds of rubbery, tire-sized curls from some unknown source littered the massive hemp strands that held the pile trees together and made walking even more difficult. Maybe the dregs of an eraser brushed off countless sheets of paper. Mysterious boulders continued to block my way and I remembered the poppy seed rolls my mother had always carried in her pockets. The woven hemp ground heaved like an earthquake and turned me completely upside down, then took on water gradually like a tough, dense sponge. I clung in fright to a ragged limb and braced myself while all began to sink into waves of rushing foam and water and, with a gentle rocking motion, through plankton, and sargasso, and beautiful languid bubbles, before settling with terrible sucking sounds into a huge trench of muck.

I sat up in bed and held still, and the dream dissolved into a feeling of afternoon sunlight and solidity that took in everything in my room, my own beloved things that I'd collected over the years as well as those few objects I'd brought with me in a grocery bag from my parents' house. I picked the Droste tin up and heard the familiar clack of buttons. Its Sister of Charity in starched wimple and black habit carried a tray on which stood an identical cocoa box with another Sister of Charity printed upon it. By this clever device a repetition of boxes with nuns holding trays of cocoa boxes appeared, each smaller than the last, until finally an infinity of smaller and smaller boxes dissolved into minuscule dots.

But what haunts me now, if I allow myself to think about it, is the cameo brooch. We couldn't even guess what might have happened to it. Janine said it probably just fell off one day and Mother never noticed. Perhaps it was stolen by one of the visiting nurses. Maybe, in her senility, Mother gave it away to a child or someone who came to the door and liked it. Or maybe, because my mother grew old and ignored it, it effaced itself. Like a stone threshold that lasts only as long as it's visited by a beggar but fades from sight at his death. I've read how a few birds, or a horse perhaps, can save the ruins of an amphitheater. A fly, a windowpane in a deserted house. A strand of hair, a brush. But I was always sad about that missing brooch. Sometimes I think if it hadn't been lost everything else would have stayed intact.

Fleurette Bleu

The gardener could make no sense of it. The gentleman was there again this morning, staring with a singular and profound intensity at the newly planted pansy beds across the graveled walk. The gardener guessed that the man was cultured from his crisp white collar and beautifully cut waistcoat. He could see it by the way the man breathed slowly in, then graciously out, as if he owned—but could be generous with—the fine spring air as he sat on the bench, his back perfectly straight, his hands folded into a neat package atop his walking stick. Yet the man's eyes did not once look up. Only his breath hesitated for a moment as if caught on some small thought. It was as if the gardener, raking the gravel into place, were only the shadow of a cloud passing over and across his path.

"So," said the doctor when his patient was recumbent on the couch. "Were you able to go to work this morning, Mr. Diesbach?"

"No . . . no I was not."

"You have been to Reiter Park."

"It's because of the pansies," Martin said, closing his eyes in order to more fully see the park.

"Go on, Mr. Diesbach."

"The plants have grown since they were put into the soil two weeks ago. Their faces have turned toward the sun."

"I see," the doctor said. To his patient the doctor's voice had a far-off quality as if distilled through the sounds of the park.

"I felt tired, even though it was morning and I had done no exercise to encourage it. I thought I would lean back on the bench, stretch my legs out, and close my eyes, but it seemed to me I did not know these particular flowers well enough to be quite as . . . informal as that. And besides, they are so young." As he said this he felt an ennui, a sudden breeze rise from the lake.

"You say you did not know them well enough?"

Martin Diesbach heard the doctor's question. Though more prominent than the question was the vision of a silken breeze playing in patterns over the grass.

"Even now I can feel the sun on my face, hear the gentle crunch of gravel, the children shouting out to each other sounding suddenly far away. The pansies were there only for me. As if I were some sort of honey-gathering insect."

"And your desire? Can you tell me about that?"

"To be close to the center, close to that place where the petals come together. A kind of message seems to rise and encircle me, and a question hangs in the air."

Sitting at her dressing table, Clara Diesbach rang for Lotte, the housemaid, three times before remembering that the girl had requested Thursdays off. She was disappointed and slightly vexed to be alone in the house with no one to talk to. And this morning when she had opened the front door and Martin had stepped out to go to work, spring, with all its inconsistencies, had seemed to rush right past her—without even asking—into the dim front hall. She would not have been able to say it as simply as this, but spring was here, and she was afraid of it.

She picked up one jeweled thing, then another, examining each in the mirror against the pleated crepon bodice of her dress, all the while talking to the cat who sat staring at her from his place on the carpet.

"Come, my little man. Come to mother, Christolph," she said. He looked at her with his green feline eyes. "Do you like this one, dear?" she asked. "Here, let mother lift you up." And she kissed his furry face as if it were the damp, pink cheek of a small child.

He curled and settled in her lap, and she turned to the mirror. The curve of her ears and the line of her jaw were particularly fine with her hair swept up and back. The blue enamel on the gold petals of the earrings glimmered as she held them in her fingers, and she was reminded of the azure color that always hung from the Virgin's shoulders, while the diamond in the center seemed to her a drop of dew, the light that shines from Christ himself. How fitting it was to her own harmony and loss, she thought sadly: Christ and his mother, waiting and indivisible within herself.

She clipped a blue-enameled flower to each ear and, with a sigh of resolve, decided she would go out and shop on the pretext of buying some new little thing—some absolute necessity—for the house; perhaps a spool of lamé thread to dangle in the sunshine of a front window for Christolph. She would tell the salesman, as she sometimes did, that she was buying it for her own child. But the thought made her suddenly tired: there was so much fatigue in pretext. The mirror showed a series of dissatisfied shadows under each eye and small, creased lines at the corners of her mouth.

A crocheted purse swung a nervous little row of strange green tassels against Lotte's skirts as she walked along the promenade next to the water. A pensioner tipped his hat as she passed. I love them all, he thought, no matter what their age. He didn't notice the tassels or anything about what she wore: what he saw was the vague shape of her breasts that appeared to move in his imagination with each step. Yet noticing a certain reluctance in her walk, he thought, no, and changed his mind: I wouldn't pick that one. She's as green as grass.

Clouds scudded against the blue, rushing off into nowhere, and she thought: just now he is at his office doing important work, not in the least thinking of me. The financial rule spins Zurich, and Zurich spins the world. He will go home, and they will have dinner together, and I will have mine in the kitchen with Greta, the cook, and not see him until tomorrow, and, even then, I may not have a moment to even glance at him in such a way that he might know. . . . But a sudden gust interrupted her favorite part—how he had said her name as if wanting something and placed his hand on her shoulder the night before as she ascended the back staircase. A sailboat in the lake suddenly listed, its billowed sail hugging tight the water, and she read its name, *Fleurette Bleu,* in a splash of fluorescent spray as it swept past. Yet how much better it all was, even in the kitchen with Greta, than eating in a farmhouse kitchen with the odor of lambs, always bleating for their mothers from a pen set up in the corner.

⌁

"The housemaid has a charming, almost childlike, habit of poising the tip of her right little finger between her lips when she's uncertain or feels she may be at fault." He crossed his ankles and covered his eyes with his forearm in thought, and the doctor suddenly saw a young man lying on spring grass, not this troubled middle-aged banker on his analyst's couch. "It's the kind of thing one learns about someone after knowing them a long time. Yet I know it's not as simple as that. It's much more. It's as Chekhov said: the soul of another is a dark forest. But the whole thing is a difficult subject. I love my wife, Clara, yet I feel a certain unease when I say the word *love*. Perhaps it's because my parents left me alone so much when I was a child. I could never get over the somewhat irrational idea that it may have been something I did or said, some way that I was, that caused them to do this. Clara was ill for several months in the first year of our marriage. We had a child that passed away at only three days old. It was a great loss to both of us. But when Clara chose to go off to a hospital in Basel, I felt it had something to do with me or the marriage, not the child's death at all. Now she has begun to put on weight, though I suppose most women eventually do that, and her clothing has become more and more elaborate. She chooses, for example, to wear a sort of peacock blue in the evening at dinner, and she rouges her lips, which I find objectionable. Also, she has certain ideas about love, certain ideas about the act. Anyway, the point is, we are Catholic."

"Yet you come to me," said the doctor, "rather than the priest and recount a story about flowers and bees and the housemaid that is somewhat fanciful—even mystical."

"And when I think of Clara's deep, yet reserved laugh it gives me pleasure and reminds me of a lovely, slightly hesitant moth. When we were first married I would tell her that." He paused as if unsure of what to think about this, and breathed a heavy sigh as if it were all too much. "I sometimes wonder what strange working of the mind chooses to bring these memories together in my thoughts."

"I have seen this in my own mind, as well," said the doctor. "I see, for example, happenings which are completely accidental, but which cluster and give meaning to my thoughts. I would never have visited my future wife at her parent's home if she had not reminded me of my own beloved Aunt Gretel."

"When I was six," Martin said, "we lived in Klein-Huningen near Basel. My father came into my room late one night and lifted me out of bed with great excitement and carried me to the porch. The sky was lit with a wonderful shimmering green toward the west. Years later I learned it was from the eruption of Krakatoa. The housemaid wears a black dress decorated with small green crescent moons on Thursdays when she goes out, and I'm suddenly reminded of Krakatoa. Yet Clara is so pleasant and uncomplaining, so good-natured, which is why I fell in love with her in the first place and knew, almost immediately, that I wanted to marry her."

"You were saying that the housemaid wears black with a design of small green crescents."

"Her face is like my mother's when she was young, rather eager and at the same time embarrassed."

Clara Diesbach stood up from her dressing table and walked over to the bed. It was all of life, she thought, that tired her so; all the things that had never been and never would be, the worry of making things appear smooth and happy, of wanting love to be something she had learned it should be as a child: immediately generous and unquestioning like slices of ripened fruit passed to someone on a clean white plate.

"You have made us for yourself," she prayed, feeling for the beads of her rosary on the bedside table, then stretching out upon the bed's down comforter. "And our heart is ever unquiet until it rests in you." When she had finished praying she got up from the bed and prepared to go out.

The house was surrounded by lindens just coming into bud. The splattered sun against the pebbled drive reminded her of brocade, the blue sky above showing here and there through the upper branches. Yet the gaiety of sun splashing on everything as the branches shifted and moved high above only seemed to remind her that life was somewhere else: with Martin and the people he worked with, women with children, the timid little housemaid who was afraid of everything and who had the day off, even the old woman, with her basket of violets, that now waddled toward her through the spring sunshine in dragging full skirts.

The old woman saw Clara hesitate with an unpleasant thought under the marble pediment of the front door where swags of fruit and roses decorated handsome Roman letters, carved to the specifications of a previous occupant, the letters read: "Summoned and not summoned God will be there." But Clara wasn't thinking about this prophesy that the oracle at Delphi had uttered when asked the outcome of a battle. After all, she passed under that pediment every day. She was thinking how preoccupied Martin had seemed of late, and she could not think what might be causing it.

⁌

"I want to take the housemaid on a day trip to Basel. Just one day might be enough to show—beyond imagination so to speak—that life offers something more than this."

"More than this?" the doctor asked. "What do you mean by more than this?"

"This yearning, this always wanting something else. When I was a child my mother took me to the museum in Basel. The stuffed animals in the tall glass cases were so natural that I thought, now we are truly in the wilds. The fox stood tense with one paw raised in expectation. The marmoset was exactly ready to swing from his ersatz branch. We looked in one case and then another until the closing bell rang, but my mother could not pull me away. When she finally tried to open the door it was locked, and I thought, good, we will build a fire to keep warm and stay for the night. We will tell stories in the dark and roast partridge on a stick. But my mother found a way for us to get out by another staircase which led through a gallery filled with marble figures. These figures were more beautiful than anything I'd ever seen, and I thought, now we have arrived. This is where we were going all along. Now we are there, this and only this is enough. Only when my mother seemed ill at ease and embarrassed did I see that the figures were completely naked."

The violet seller's eyes settled on Lotte gazing at a sailboat in the distance. The towers of the old town beyond the harbor stood out sharply against the hill whose crest curved like the protection of an arm above it. A cloud swept across the sun, and Lotte shivered in her strange, old-fashioned dress. The old woman thought, she'll be poor and yearning her whole life away. Those kind always are. Yearning to rise above herself and forgetting her hat or jacket or some other thing that would help to make her warm or comfortable.

Lotte pondered what to do next, still nagged, as she had been in the back of her mind all morning, by the memory of asking Mrs. Diesbach for an increase. She had been refused on the grounds that she had not been with them long enough. Greta the cook, she had been told, had been with them three years and seemed happy enough. She thought now that she should have asked Mr. Diesbach himself since he had made every indication that there was something he wanted from her. Yet Mrs. Diesbach had made it clear that it was she who ran the house. "If there is anything you need," she said, "you must come to me. Above all, do not bother Mr. Diesbach. He has enough to worry about at his office."

Now the surface of the lake was ragged with whitecaps, and the little sailboats in the distance all headed toward the dock. The quay where she stood was bathed in shadow while the sails in the distance caught the sun like so many white, windblown petals. She turned to move on and saw an old woman struggling with a basket of violets, and she thought, dear Lord, save me from becoming as poor and ragged and ugly as that.

Clara Diesbach thought if she saw no one to talk to she might stop and rest a moment in the comforting, baroque peace of St. Peter's Church. Happily, she saw a child and nursemaid from down the street walking toward her.

The nursemaid saw her coming and took the child's hand. "Come now, darling, cross over," she said. "We don't want you all grabbed up and crushed."

Clara could see, as they crossed the street and avoided her, that the child's straw hat was tied with a streaming pink ribbon. A bunch of silk cornflowers tied at the knot on the back bobbed as the child pointedly ignored Clara and skipped past.

"Well," said the doctor, "our time is up."

Martin Diesbach breathed a deep sigh. He didn't like being wrenched from his dreams and memories into the sterile and denying present. The room had grown dark as if it were about to rain. Beyond the doctor, comfortably sitting with a notepad in his chair, and between the dark velvet curtains, tiny round buds quivered like beads in the wind. The doctor smiled a knowing and completely comfortable smile. His eyes behind his steel-rimmed spectacles conveyed affection as well as respect. He reached to his desk cluttered with small votive objects and picked up one in particular.

"You see," he said, "the Egyptian god Horus. He carries the sun above his head. Just as you do, Mr. Diesbach. The American Pueblos worship the sun, also. They believe their worship at dawn secures the sun's rising not just for them but for the whole world. They believe if they abandon the sun it would only be a matter of days before it would completely extinguish."

Martin Diesbach held the little statue with the jackal's head, thin body, the flat disk of sun held by upraised arms, and looked at it thoughtfully before handing it back to the doctor. Then he took up his cane and put on his hat.

"It is good—even efficacious—to be a part of everything: stones, trees, clouds, and water. I'll see you next week, Mr. Diesbach," the doctor said. "And remember the words of Hölderlin: where there is danger there is also salvation."

Martin Diesbach walked down the Bahnhofstrasse through the noonday crowd. The day was warm enough when the sun swept aside the clouds. And something like a premonition was in the air. All the passing faces were so different and unique, yet all the same and hard to fix. There up ahead was the jewelry shop where he'd bought the blue enamel earrings he'd given his wife last Christmas. Suddenly the well-defined and ample figure of his wife came clear to him as she peered intently into the window of the shop. His first impulse was to say hello, yet seeing her he felt a tugging guilt and thought better of it. I'd only feel I had to buy her something expensive, he thought.

He walked on quickly until the street opened into the wide promenade of the Mythenquai beyond the wharf. A crone approached, and her basket, stacked with tightly bound nosegays, seemed a kind of portent. He bought a nosegay, yet out by the water watching the sailboats breezing in to dock, he suddenly had no idea what to do with it. It was this sudden strange absence of purpose connected to the violets that had been his undoing, he later told the doctor. For just at the moment he was about to toss the violets into the water and have them float away with a kind of pleasurable regret, the housemaid appeared in the distance shivering and hugging herself for warmth in her green moon dress. She turned to face him, and he walked toward her, as a leathery flap of pigeons rose and caught the light and sailed off. In one great curving arc they changed direction, then, with a wave of gleaming feathers, the sun catching the crest, they floated softly down to earth. Martin, far away as he still was, thought he saw an infinite light gleam and beckon in the housemaid's open pupils.

The doctor said nothing. Now, between the curtains, the fruit tree's buds had opened into diffuse puffs.

"Afterward, after we left the hotel—separately of course—we walked along the quay and a strange feeling of fate seemed present. We walked as naturally as if we had been made for each other. She had an expression of shyness—almost admiration in her face. But strangest of all—and I don't quite know how to say this—I realized that she had appeared in my life just as my need had created an opening for her." He turned his head and looked at the doctor. "My life seems such an odd tale to me: each new thing disappearing into the past to make room for the next."

"I have often thought," said the doctor, "that one day I

might attempt to write a memoir. Yet when I think of life as we live it, I see that all its coalescing then disintegrating parts would never fit between the pages of a book."

Martin Diesbach closed his eyes. Somewhere in the reaches of the doctor's house he heard a child singing a nursery verse, and the figure of the housemaid appeared before him, beaming and hopeful as she had been before they parted.

After his patient had gone, the doctor moved to his desk. A Buddha on a lotus leaf, surrounded by a sliver of moon and bowers of cloud, covered the wall behind him so that the maid, entering with his afternoon pot of chocolate and seeing the doctor, with stark white hair and finely wrinkled face, giving her a smile and rising to a stand to help her with the tray, suddenly saw the doctor's head surrounded by clouds, the moon hanging on one side and the Buddha seated on the other.

The doctor lifted his pen in thought. "Every patient is a separate tale," he wrote, "in which there exists innumerable possibilities as well as infinite, binding constraints." He gazed at his library in thought. Each book, with its tiny round white label, was shelved and indexed against the walls. His own father had once had just such a library, a wonderful paneled room crowded with books about everything under the sun. The sun and beyond, he thought. Yes, the sun and beyond. Yet even at age six or seven he had climbed up the library ladder and opened those books, understanding only the smallest part. Now, in adulthood, the mysteries were all still there, had become not only expected but requisite, so that only the inexplicable—Faust's untreadable regions, that unknown which brooked no human intervention—seemed to hold his love and his interest.

Lotte awoke in her third-floor bedroom, cranked open the window sash, and the image of her employer making love to her in the hotel room suddenly came back.

"Do you know," he had asked her when he finally spoke, "what they say about the bees?" But now, standing by her window, she could not remember what he had given as the answer after she had shaken her head. The image of him lying next to her naked under the sheet shrank from her mind and wouldn't stay fixed. She was in love and she knew it, yet his body had been a disappointment to her, the act strangely unfulfilling and unpleasant. Not at all what she had wished.

After breakfast she saw him take something from his coat pocket, and examine it with mild surprise before placing it on the hall table. Nothing more than a smudge of purple and green, it was: a crushed and wilted violet. He stood there with his hat on, and she, all prim in her apron, handed him his walking stick. Mrs. Diesbach kissed him on the cheek, then picked a long, curling hair from his lapel. She held it at arm's length as if she were holding the tail of a tiny dead rat. And everything hung at that moment between the three of them like a high and fragile drop of water suspended from the rocky overhang of a precipice.

"Where did this come from?" Mrs. Diesbach asked. Then she let go of the hair and watched it float to the floor.

"The wind, no doubt," he said, and, giving his wife a superfluous kiss on the cheek, stepped out into the clear morning and walked off.

That night Lotte dreamed she was a bird flying above an endless ocean. The sun sparkled on the shifting water below making strange and beautiful patterns like sequined scarves, and she thought, I will fly on forever. It is my fate and my joy

Fleurette Bleu

to fly on forever. To travel hopefully is a far better thing than to ever arrive. Yet no sooner had she thought this than her wings grew heavy and tired, and she was seized with fright, for no one had taught her how to glide into a floating position on the surface of the water. She awoke for a moment in relief and the dream erased, but as soon as she'd fallen asleep again, a castle rose from the waters, and she recognized it as the ruined castle of Stein that she'd visited so many times with her father. Its oaken wood door banged with the wind on its salt-rusted hinges, open, then shut; open, then shut. Waves sprayed into arcs and merged with her breath, and she thought in the dream, one no longer needs the eyes of a dove to see where they are. The shutters on the small tower window banged open in the wind, and a jeweled hand reached out to still her flight, the fingers heavy with rings and grown languid and thick. . . .

But in the light of day she went about her work, and the lover's great peace, that one side of the double bargain, descended upon her. Even when Mrs. Diesbach suggested, in a voice that had grown strangely aloof, that she change the hall flowers, or asked would she please think about hanging the summer curtains, or polish the serving pieces, time seemed to stand still. She walked from one room to the next with her feather duster and rags and furniture wax, watching sunlight fall across the carpets, skimming the surface of thoughts, regretting nothing, wishing for nothing, not even thinking to hold her breath for what might come next.

Yet when she closed her eyes to dream at night, there was the thick, jeweled hand poised above the water, and no help in sight. And Mr. Diesbach? Except for Thursdays between two and four, he hardly seemed to recognize her.

"In the dream I had grown quite old," he said. "I wore antique clothes and boots all made of coarse leather. There was a great storm of a terrible dark color that beat the waves into huge crests against the rocks. It gave everything a wild impasto look, the way a curled lock of hair or the fold of a jacket looks in a painting, in a Rembrandt for example, if you stand up close to inspect it. Far out to sea, though I couldn't see it but knew with certainty it was there, a castle waited for me upon an island of rock. I held to the rope of a small boat that tossed mercilessly in the water, and I saw, then, that my wife stood beside me on the shore as if I were supposed to help her in some way. Yet for some reason unknown to me I could not reach out to her, and she had to climb into the bow alone. She sat there holding a package tied in coarse cloth in her lap, and I saw that she was young and her clothes simple and dark. And I knew then for certain that I would be responsible for rowing her out."

"And you yourself?" asked the doctor. "Were you not to stay with her in this castle?"

"I don't know. I don't know at all. Perhaps I was to row back to it later."

The doctor cleared his throat, and his patient was suddenly brought back.

"What am I to do?" Martin Diesbach asked.

Christolph, the cat, raised his head, registering the fact that Clara, her rosary wound through her fingers, was still deep into her afternoon nap. She was dreaming a dream that would vanish, as all her dreams did, the moment she woke up. But for now it was vivid enough as she sat in the bow of a small rowboat holding fast to a package tied in rough cloth in her lap. An aged man strained at the oars, and the wind blew fresh and clear as if a storm had just passed. And she wondered, why do the eyes of old men always seem to recede into their pasts? They came to a castle whose door swung open with a great silent creak completely by itself. How strange, she thought as she stepped inside, a door that opens to a circular staircase inside a tower and at the top a perfectly round room with only one window to look out of. But I'm so hungry and tired of climbing these steps, she thought as she entered the perfectly round room. The window's casement was the length of her forearms as she bent her elbows and leaned on her arms to see out. Far below the old man rowed away from her, becoming smaller and smaller, while in the great distance of blue, a dove with perfectly incised silver feathers, each attached to its body by a tiny hinge, spoke in the unintelligible voice of a child.

Christolph saw that his mistress was waking up, for Clara sighed and murmured in her sleep as if in disappointment, then turned and tossed her skirts aside with an impatient foot. She lay there staring at the ceiling for a long time, trying to puzzle her life out. Especially bothersome to her was the incident connected with the jewelry shop: Martin had looked the other way, rushed on, and pretended not to see her. He had never done such a thing before; he had always seemed pleased when their paths had crossed. And now the silly housemaid always tried to place herself in front of him.

"My wife," he said, "may not be completely aware, but she knows something is amiss. It hangs between us like a phantom in the house. She hardly rings for the housemaid now, but prefers to do all sorts of things herself. And it's Thursday, of course, the day for my weekly appointment with the housemaid by the boat dock."

"You were saying you thought your wife knew about the affair."

"She was playing with the cat after dinner. The cat was jabbing at a wooden spool of thread with his paw and making it roll across the wood floor between the carpets and my wife said to me as I read the evening gazette, 'The Lord speaks to us in so many ways, Martin.' She said this as if musing. It is not unusual for her to say such things. Then she said, 'You know, Martin, I love the sound of wood rolling against wood that the cat makes when he plays.' And I said something or other so as not to be rude, and then I heard her say, 'I think it's because you're here with me. If I lived without you—or with anyone else—I would not love the sound that spool makes half as much. Perhaps I would even grow to hate it.' It was as if her words were completely expected, as if all along I'd had a premonition—almost a desire—that she would say something like this. Perhaps that's why. . . ."

"Yes?"

"Perhaps that's why I arranged to see the housemaid only once a week. Perhaps that's why she's given notice. Yet what could my reasons have been for walking with her in public as if wanting my wife to find out? And this morning I passed the same crone selling violets on the Bahnhofstrasse. She held out a nosegay and said, 'For your fledgling, sir!' and I became suddenly ashamed, for it was as if the whole world knew the lessons of my heart. It was at that moment, with that strange happening by pure chance, that I knew my meetings with the housemaid would end. I will not be there this afternoon to meet her. I feel I've disappointed her in some way, and that she, too, will not be there watching the boats by the water."

"One often sees this acausal connecting principal," said the doctor kindly. "Especially in matters of the heart."

"It's as if the solution has appeared of its own accord," said Martin, "almost out of nature."

Lotte had stripped the bed, and her small suitcase was packed full and shut and lying on the mattress. Her clock had been packed since midday along with everything else. It was now late afternoon, but one needed no clock to see that: sun drenched the wall above the bed liquefying the ordinary roses of the wallpaper to a dream gone stale and melted, a dream in which she had been the mistress of a great and beautiful house with adoring husband and children to go with it. Her father had promised to come in from Baden on the train and pick her up. He had not wanted her to work for people in the city in the first place.

She sat on the edge of the bed trying to remember the way her father looked, the way the road curved through the fields, then bent sharply through a copse of birch toward the barn and house. She tried to imagine it as she wanted it to be: filled with light like a cup of milk.

She heard the crunch of farm boots on gravel and knew immediately that it was the determined step of her father. She could remember no other details in that moment, no specifics, but knew that soon she must. How beautiful things could be with imagination. Even the ordinary and repetitious became lovely and frivolous. How quickly it will soon be past, she thought. How quickly it will all dissolve into the blue of dusk.

Provenance

"When are you sending Mother's pearls?" I say over the phone from New York to Paris, deliberately stringing the words out like each pearl itself over the great Atlantic so my elderly father will be sure to hear and understand exactly what it is I mean and want. "The ones you sent are fakes, Dad, you know that."

He says nothing. Nothing about the way he's wrapped a costume jewelry pearl necklace that I've never seen before in old tissue paper, then sent it in place of the original all the way from Paris in an old glove box.

"Did you hear me?" I ask, imagining him a skeletal bird of prey standing next to the phone table in his apartment foyer in Paris.

"Hear that?" he asks, turning my question back upon itself. "It's Madame Bottin's Pekin dog yelping and defecating in the courtyard. He's growing a wart like a huckleberry on his nose. Pretty soon it will obliterate the whole damn dog. He woke me up at dawn again this morning."

Then his words drown in static, and I hear only the heaving great Atlantic over which our voices course in brittle, grainy waves of sound, minutely small but physically electric. Outside my apartment a jackhammer starts. They're laying fiber-optic cable the width of a tree trunk under the sidewalk.

Something for cell phones or computers I guess. I move over to the window with the phone in my hand and try—without success—to shut it. My father's voice emerges through it all.

"Your mother said in a dream last night just before I woke up, I'll love you forever, Victor, promise you'll never change, and in the dream I promised her. So much for promises. In the beginning your mother adored me. She said, you'll get tired of me, Vic, like lovers do, and you know what I said?"

"Yes, I do, Dad, yes, I do, I know exactly what you said, you've told me before." And I steel myself against his recurrent vision of my poor deceased mother by imagining the waters of the great North Atlantic.

Night rises over the waves thick and starless and black with only the vaguest point of light from a ship in the far distance off Montauk Point. Across those miles of ocean the cliffs of Dover appear as the first landfall in a dawn that's only an intimation of light itself. The sound of the jackhammer is momentarily replaced by rap music from a passing car. Words float heavy and disparaging as lead into the distance.

"Soit belle," my father tells me, quoting Baudelaire, "and soit triste. Be beautiful and sad, Daughter."

"You carry them around in your coat pocket like a rosary, Dad. What good are they in your pocket?"

"She looked at me in the dream, and her eyes, lit by a shaft of sun, were the perfect color of quince," my father says, "that Robertson's quince jam she used to like for breakfast."

With that proxy called memory my father has decided that my mother's brown eyes were the golden color of quince. He decided also long ago that my mother and I should not be friends. Resentment against the intrusive third party, I guess.

I saw the pearls when I visited last Christmas, also the letter Mrs. Weems wrote when she sent them to my father in

Paris. In their stained state they looked nothing like they had on my parents' wedding night when my father waited until my mother had completely undressed before lifting her weight of hair and hanging them around her neck. They were moist, he always insists on telling me, from the oyster, just like your mother was. He always tells me more than I want or need to know, more than a daughter is comfortable with.

I stand in my apartment and stare at a Gateway black-and-white packing box in the middle of the living room floor. I'm trying not to imagine the linings of my father's pockets worn thin with small holes, my mother's pearls slipping through, falling into a gutter filled with curling fall leaves and cigarette butts, carried away by the next good autumn rain into the malodorous sewers of Paris.

The letter from Mrs. Weems, once a perfectly fresh and ordinary-looking letter in an airmail envelope, was a grayed scrap, when I saw it last Christmas, on which barely legible words were written with a ballpoint in precise, outdated penmanship: "Your wife Anna Brendt-Morrison," it read, "died in her sleep on September 24. I send these to you because I've misplaced your daughter's address. With sincere good wishes, Alice Weems, 1305A Grant."

Two untruths here. One, my mother did not die in her sleep; she died of a heart attack on a bus. I suppose Mrs. Weems felt it was better to die in a bed than a bus. Dying in her sleep would have been too comfortable for my mother, a woman so full of energy and affection and remorse. The other untruth: Mrs. Weems had my address right there next to my father's in her little cardboard book. She just didn't like me because she thought I didn't go down to Richmond enough.

"Je suis la plaie et le couteau," my father says, "the wound and the knife."

That's for sure. Perhaps if I said nothing he would decide to send them, but I know this is probably the least likely scenario. The unopened packing box with its black and white motif sits in the center of the floor. As a design element in the room it definitely doesn't work. It just takes over. In the back of my mind is a vague plan to open it.

"They're repairing the sewer on Rue Saint Daru," my father says. "Impossible to get through what with the noise and trucks. I'm not walking all the way around, not with my knees." Yet he'd go through hell and high water before canceling a date with his friend Father Frank Fahey, the man he calls the good father.

"Why are you so indebted to him?" I ask.

"He understands," my father says, "and he needs me to help him plan for some renovations to the Virgin's niche."

I see my father winding his way through the narrow streets toward Father Fahey, who sits waiting for him at Arnaud's, their favorite café across from Saint Joseph's. On the way he climbs the steps of the little White Russian church on Newski Hill, as he calls it, to sit and watch the icons blacken with smoke. He likes to edge his way into weddings and baptisms and funerals and stand against the back wall; he likes to watch the shivering babies sprinkled with holy water, the brides with their innocence gone weeks and months before, the grooms not knowing what they're getting into. He likes the intimacy of lives from a distance. I see him pretending he's a member of the family, a part of the invited crowd. Then he continues down Avenue Hoche, shuffling through the curling leaves smelling of musk and mold, their own slowly pulverizing tobacco.

"To be understood is all I ask," he says to me. His voice cracks with self-pity.

"They ought to be worn," I tell him.

He is silent, and I hear nothing but static, as if way out at sea it has started to rain on the surface of the water.

"I have told Father Fahey my problem," my father finally says, "and I have heard his. He needs five thousand dollars for the gold leaf to decorate the Virgin's niche."

"You're not giving it to him are you?" Not that my father can't well afford it. Not that I need it.

He pauses. "Quelle est cette ile triste et noir?" he asks.

But I imagine no sad black island myself, only the heaving tides of the ocean that separates us and the pearls that bind us, and his head with the skin clinging to his skull, the hollow cheeks sagging gray from the skeletal cheekbones as he talks. And Father Fahey, who I now know is a crook. Perhaps if I were to actually unpack my new computer—which arrived two weeks ago and is still in the Holstein box—and write my father a letter explaining just how I feel. . . .

"C'est Cythère," he says, "they tell us a country famous in song, banal Eldorado of all the old bachelors. Reminds me of the good Father and myself."

I see the two of them at their table by the window. They are enveloped by a damp glow. Outside the air rings with a new Parisian fall. Father Fahey talks to my father, and a sort of cunning coats his words as they slide from his lips. Yet my father is protected by these words; they give him a sense of solace. Careful and tremulous and waiting to spill, my father lifts his thick little coffee cup.

"He drinks too much scotch," my father says. "He talks about original sin and his sweet, proud Virgin of the Magnificat, how she deserves more than he can possibly give her. He tells me what a good position I'm in to help. When he's had too much scotch he lifts his glass and shouts, 'Garçon! Un autre . . . —s'il vous plaît! Un autre!'"

My father's imitation, though robust, rings with a kind of lugubrious loss. I imagine the glass in Father Fahey's sinewy hand coming down with a kind of calculated emphasis. I imagine him looking hard at my father for effect. Money can never heal wounds, Father Fahey says. No, no, of course not, my father answers, it only buys the poultice.

"An impossible situation for him," continues my father. "He calls her love beneficent, always living, always consecrating."

He pauses, not to hear my answer, which he doesn't care about, but to shift to a succeeding thought.

"What am I to do?" he asks as if I'm supposed to help. "Your mother's eyes on me every night, accusing me like she did when it all came out."

"When what came out?" I ask.

"You know Baudelaire's theory of true civilization, Daughter?" my father asks. "Have I told you that? True civilization, the diminution of the traces of original sin?"

And it strikes me as I hear his thought through the medium of Baudelaire, in a way more precise than he could ever say it himself, that my father isn't senile at all, he's just caught. My living room seems placed around the Gateway box. The box has a mug sitting on it that I won a long time ago in a race. The mug, half-full of cold coffee, says in red block letters, "Palisades 10 K." Two Miro posters hang on opposite walls. Sofa and chairs, modern and trim and flat, are relieved only by a pair of throw pillows sewn from Mexican fabric. The television is a rectangle of staring black. For a moment my heart and mind want to be in my father's elegant and shabby sitting room on the Boulevard de Courcelles stacked with piles and piles of crumb-stained books, littered with ineffective mousetraps, draped with ancient, unraveling sweaters and scarves. And I know, as I sit there listening to my father, that in our own way we're both caught.

All his high-ceilinged rooms with their towering windows and dusty period moldings could open, if he so chose, like Pandora's box onto the crisp late fall, the carousel and chestnut trees yellowing into gold, the Punch and Judy and screaming, laughing children of Parc Monceau. If he so chose. Which he does not. Rather he sits and reads *Fleur du Mal* with his feet on the tapestry of a concave ottoman and tries to connect Baudelaire with everything he is capable of seeing within himself. Mère des souvenirs, maîtresse des maîtresses, he says to himself as the words fade, and he starts awake, trying to fish a translation out of the deep sea of his thoughts. Mother of memories, mistress of mistresses, he tells himself, hooking the words and drawing them in with a smooth, slow line as his head nods onto his chest, as his lips hang flaccid, and his lids drop.

"It snowed all night," he tells me in his next call. "I looked down into the street and your mother's eyes like Russian amber looked at me out of the snow as it fell. Then I looked at her breasts and the pearls gleamed on her chest as if they were the snow itself."

I imagine a gap of tattered fringe behind him as he says this, a slash of glaring snow.

"Are you coming for Christmas, Daughter?" he asks.

"I can't." My voice is matter-of-fact. I'd gone last Christmas and that was enough.

"I'll go to mass at Saint Joseph's, maybe have dinner with

the good father. Do you want a present of some kind?" he asks.

"Funny you should mention it."

For this indulgent bit of cheek I hang momentarily aloft waiting for a forgiving parental flash.

"There are in every man, at every hour," my father says, "two simultaneous postulations. One toward God, the other toward Satan. But to be a saint for one's self . . . ah, there's the rub. You wouldn't understand this, Daughter, but it's Father Fahey who's helping me to do that."

"How?" I ask. "How is he helping you to do that? You know he's a crook don't you, Dad?"

"The sanctity of penance in the form of gift."

I see Father Fahey's fingers caressing the wad of bills my father always carries in his pocket. His eyes are like the corners of old fireplaces, full of dying ash. Yet the sight of my father's thick donation is the lifting gust that brings them to life, the glowing, petulant spark. I imagine the priest emptying another glass of scotch, taking an anxious but satisfying drag of his cigarette and pocketing both my father's wad of bills and his matches.

"I've told him about the pearls," my father says. "What was I to do quand le ciel est bas et lourd? With such a low and heavy sky what is one to do? Heh, Daughter?" he asks. "In those days one's wedding night was the first. A man had to be tender, of course, but what is one to do with the aggression of sex? Deep into the mystery as Baudelaire would have put it. Hard to believe she loved me once. But of course the pearls are proof of that. I hid them for reasons I hardly now remember," he confesses. "Perhaps I thought she'd stopped loving me. . . .—Hear that?" he asks. "It's Madame Bottin's damned

Pekin dog. First thing I see when I walk into the courtyard is his crabbed yellow signature in the snow. She ought to call him Buster Pollock. The good father keeps a picture postcard of the Virgin in his pocket. He shows it to everyone he meets as if she were his lady friend. Did I tell you that?"

"Well, she'll never disappoint him," I say.

"She stands on a cloud," he tells me, "in a blue robe, a penumbra of gold behind her head."

I see Father Fahey handing the postcard to my father.

"Je suis le plait et le couteau," my father says, "the blow and the cheek, the limbs and the wheel, the knife and the wound. She stopped loving me so I, the victim, became the executioner. So to speak . . . ," my father says. "So to speak."

Father Fahey encourages all of this from my father, I know, probably even pouring his own scotch into my father's half-filled coffee cup with a generous but desultory flourish.

"That Algerian is another one," my father says. "He stands outside Arnaud's dawn to dusk. The sleeves of his coat are so short it looks like someone's cut them off. Completely lost," he says. "Completely lost. The good father says Sanctus and makes the sign of the cross whenever we pass, but he never buys any chestnuts. Neither do I for that matter. The good father says no one's truly religious—especially himself."

I remember the Algerian from last Christmas. He'd removed the charcoal with a metal scoop from a hole in the side of his oil drum and dumped it into the twilight snow. Then he'd proceeded to dump the few remaining blackened chestnuts. They had sunk, I was sure even then from inside the café, with an infinitesimal hiss. They had suddenly become the buckeyes, as I sat there at that table with my father, which had littered the sidewalk outside my mother's Richmond boardinghouse.

I see Father Fahey leaning close to my father at that same table at Arnaud's, his stale breath commingling with my father's, his eyes red with avarice. My Lady of the Magnificat, he says tragically, my beautiful Lady of the Magnificat, how I have disappointed her, and a drop of gleaming spittle falls onto the stained table from his lower lip.

"Of course I confessed to him," my father tells me across the Atlantic.

"What did you confess?" I ask.

"I confessed I'd hidden your mother's pearls under the front seat of the car."

I see Father Fahey's head trembling, anticipating the always remunerative results of guilt.

"I told him she'd reported the theft to the police, then the insurance company," my father says with a sigh of remorse. "Of course when she first found them I told her it was your fault. You were only ten so it didn't matter. But she didn't believe me, so I went ahead and confessed."

The news of this betrayal is momentarily strange and awful to me, yet it fits in perfectly with my father. I imagine him sitting at that little table with Father Fahey and lifting my mother's pearls from his pocket. Father Fahey starts to reach out to them, then thinks better of it. Lying there, surrounded by a pack of Gauloise and a book of matches, my father's coffee dregs in his little white cup, and Father Fahey's glistening and immutable scotch on the rocks, the pearls are, as I imagine them, one sad disappointment knotted to another. They are as stained and yellow as they were last Christmas with Brilcream and sweat, the brown of tobacco, the butter from innumerable pains au chocolat.

"I've lost the tip off my cane," he tells me. "It's snowing too hard to go out. I went out yesterday and almost fell."

A gleam behind him touches the enamel face of the ormolu clock, which strikes across the waters like a toast rung on the thin rim of a lone champagne glass.

"Les parfums, les couleurs, les sons se répondent, they echo one another," he says, savoring the sound. He picks the telephone base up, and I hear him shuffling somewhere with it.

"Where are you going?" I ask him, for the thin needle of clock strike has stitched together a series of random and half-lit, floating and gathering thoughts. And I suddenly see Father Fahey walking off into the snow with my pearls in his pocket.

"I'm winding the chimes back up," my father says, his voice melting into diffuse, hard static.

"There is no moral progress except in the individual by the individual himself," my father says. "Baudelaire was well aware of this, Daughter, as are the good father and myself."

Father Fahey's sinewy hand reaches into his own coat pocket.

"My God," I say in disbelief. "You gave my pearls to Father Fahey. You gave my pearls to him, didn't you Dad?"

"Il n'existe que trois êtres respectables," he says, "only three things worthy of respect, Daughter: le prètre, le guerrier, le poète. Savoir, tuer, et creer. Most important is the poet—to create, but second is the priest—to know."

For a long moment I disappear in an aching kind of liquid loss, a tired hot remorse, for all the times I never visited my mother, never could get past the different selves that were the two of us, the subtle—and not so subtle—wedges my father used to keep us apart. I am that picture, for one brief moment, of the patient in her dull sack dress and bare feet drawn up on a cheap wooden bench in some locked ward. It is this brief near death, this great pain, which is a letting go. And it occurs to me, as the woman on the bench shifts her body and looks up, that maybe I should hang up the phone and let my father be. But I don't, of course, because I still hope for the only thing of value my mother left.

"It may be Christmas," he tells me next time we talk, "but I'm not going anywhere. I took one step out into the snow and had to turn back."

I see him caught against the massive courtyard gate like a piece of blown scrap. He's yearning to be back upstairs in the safety of his bath, his tub of hot water on four lion's paws, his bed with its unchanged sheets. In a moment of sudden hope I wonder if he's really given my pearls to Father Fahey after all, or if he's simply trying to mislead me again so he can keep them for himself.

The shade glows over his book. The Louis Quinze headboard is covered with shredded pink silk, though this silk darkened by smoke from my father's cigarettes has nothing to do with my mother, it opens for me the vision of her redbud-in-bloom lipstick trespassing the boundary of her creased lips, the chipped lipstick cylinder in the bottom of the purse still clutched to her chest when they tried to revive her on that bus. The pearls would have been back in her room, I think, in her bedside table or top dresser drawer. I can't remember her wearing them once after my father left. By habit I reach for the mug on the Holstein packing box, but the box—even the room itself—has faded to a mute shadow of its former self.

But my father's as clear to me in his striped pajamas with the bulging knees, the slippers he calls pantoufles, as if I were standing by his side. For a moment I imagine my pearls as a transvestite's gaudy necklace hanging loosely around his neck. He's bending over the old gas oven in his massive unrenovated kitchen to remove his pain au chocolat. He's left it, as always, too long. It falls from his hands onto the floor, and he jabs with a long meat fork to pick it up as the pearls dangle and swing obscenely from his neck. The pastry is like the edges of old newspapers, *Le Monde* and the *Herald Tribune,* which he uses as kindling to start his fires. It flakes onto the worn stone floor.

Yet even as he sleeps folded inward like some prehistoric bird my mind flies from one pocket and drawer, one corner of his apartment to the next. Above his silent and nagging dreams of my mother, shadows hover on the walls with the fluidity and stillness of ancient waters. But the pearls are no longer in his coat nor around his neck, nor on the bedside stand, nor in any drawer. He dreams his dreams close to the surface where my sweet, bitter, recalcitrant mother tells him, Victor, I shall love you forever. Victor, she says to him one more time, looking at him steadily for emphasis, I shall love you forever.

I cross the snowy street devoid of traffic and move along the lanceate railing of the park. It is unclear to me as I imagine this whether I should hide or be seen, whether I will hail Father Fahey and make my demands, call for a policeman and accuse him of fraud, insist he is no priest at all but a common crook. It is unclear to me as my imagination moves down Avenue Hoch, through the Alleé Comtesse de Ségur, along Avenue Van Dyck with its lovely carved facades, the house with the dolphin rainwater spouts, whether when I find him I will stop him at all or will bide my time and wait for just the right moment to steal the pearls back.

I can see him now in the distance, his black coat and fedora against the snow. He has paused at the corner of Avenue Van Dyck to search deep in his pockets. His eyes gleam and his back softly curves as if he's touched a woman's sex, and I shudder at this as his face glows with the mystery of it.

Snow swirls and eddies and floats around us as he moves off, and I follow him toward Saint Joseph's. It muffles our footsteps. Breathless powder clings to the sleeves of his black wool coat, catches in fine white grains on the brim of his black felt hat. Up ahead the facade of Saint Joseph's holds handfuls of white new-fallen snow as if it were a cliff where swallows dwelt. He approaches the wide steps while his right hand gently plays in his pocket. Yet before I can even imagine it he's slipped away from me through the doors of the church.

He makes his way between the massive columns that flank the aisle moving quietly over the worn stone floor. He slows as he turns to go down the south transept, and I speed up. And then—as I almost reach him—I see the niche. Twisting tails and tongues and leering lips, the entrails of a thousand tiny serpents swim around its Gothic arch. Yet I see as I approach that these are but gold-leafed buds, the intertwined leaves and stems, the petals and stamens of flowers.

He stands before her with his head bowed. The years have grayed the once blue plaster of her gown, the drape on her head, the gathered, white frill around her neck. Her arms are poised above him in benediction, I think—or perhaps supplication—it's hard to tell, for imagination catches sometimes with moments of unknowing, tiny inadvertent blanks in which one stops and waits to see which way the mind would prefer for something to work out.

One palm with its chipped finger turns up and the other turns down. Father Fahey removes the pearls from his pocket and raises them toward her with both hands as if to fasten them around her neck, but she is too tall to reach as she rises above him gazing into the immeasurable distance, and he is too short.

For a long moment he looks at her in contemplation wondering what to do next. Her full peasant face is expectant, yet her stance, the way the drapery falls and rests exhausted at her feet, seems molded from some deep regret. The iris of each eye is held and fixed with a circle of chestnut paint, the pupils a tiny half-moon carved out, yet they appear living and black. He takes a shuffling step toward her. Then he bends his head and brings the pearls to his mouth and covers them with a devout wet kiss. My hand is to his shoulder now, and I touch him on the back, but he steps quickly forward, and my hand—which he has not felt—stays poised and alert. He reaches up to place the pearls in her upturned palm and suddenly I see her cheeks blush. Her lips part, and the moisture on a tooth catches the light. He holds a moment as if gazing right through her into the far distance. Then he bends in adoration and gives her sandled foot a kiss.

Night-Blooming Cereus

The child, in her fancy Sunday dress, wandered the rooming house halls, spying for the interest and instruction of it. She touched a hand to Mary Catton's door, wanting the housekeeper to wake up, yet not wanting to be held responsible, as she waited for her mother, three doors down the hall, to put on her face for church.

Mary Catton slept, because the child had not knocked—only touched—and the door stayed closed. Yet the child knew Mary Catton well enough to see through the door: see the faintly cool morning light, how still it lay on all the sewing things that the housekeeper, in playful conspiracy, had explained to her when the child was guest. She could see Mary Catton sleeping: a woman in those brief years before the flesh goes slack, the housekeeper was completely still like a sleek fish sleeping at the bottom of a languid pool of clear water.

Ah, the child thought in symbol more than word, for the words did not yet belong to her that could always and naturally express what she knew and felt: that the rooming house would let go of her small self, that the ripple of Mary Catton's dreams would reflect on the ceiling, flicker in the thickening summer light, reduce a green apple on the bedside table that the child had given her the day before to a kind of spectral shape the way deep summer softens and debauches, causes fruit to suddenly show a circle of rot, paints with reluctance things that deserve importance: the spools of red darning thread stacked in a pile, the pincushion stuck with needles, the tiny fine-point embroidery scissors, the stiff, carefully folded shirts covered with red embroidery ready to be delivered to Colonel Kramer. Mary Catton would awaken and rise to wash and dress and then embroider, then after church, the house would take the child back.

And she saw Mary Catton's face, a face she couldn't turn away from, because, even in sleep, it held her with something wordless, something she might not have heard before. The soles of Mary Catton's feet were dark with dirt, her rear was softly pale and dimpled, she lay on her side, one arm tossed over the other, hair strangely askew. Saturday night's makeup has run from her eyes onto her cheeks. Ah, the dark goddess of morning! is what the child would think if she were standing next to Mary Catton's bed and had the words.

The child's still, dark eyes peeked through the open slit in Jack Brockman's door as he lay thinking on his bed and settled on his hair, which was so thin it resembled small India ink lines drawn unevenly across the top of his head.

Every day but Sunday he stood in the hot sun, wiping his forehead with a handkerchief on the corner of Shelby and English by a card table covered with a black cloth from which he sold fancy, badly constructed guitars—though he knew little or nothing of music—because he'd gotten a deal on a hundred from a man named Delaney, whom he'd met in a bar. He was lying on his bed in his frequently repaired underwear, his only pair. He was particularly fond of them: they had belonged to his father. Also, not bequeathed, but left behind by his deceased father, a tin cigarette lighter in the shape of a dancing girl with the word *Hawaii* neatly spread across her

Night-Blooming Cereus

buttocks, a pair of gradually loosening suspenders, and two knit ties of indeterminate color.

Every day is a brand-new place, he thought optimistically, his eyes to the ceiling as he smoked a cigarette, even though you might be in the very same location, you never knew what might transpire. This was given to himself as reason to stay right where he was in Minneapolis until the fall, not pull up stakes immediately and travel. He exhaled a thin stream of smoke as he thought about it. Yet how could it be, he wondered with sudden bored pessimism, when every day, no matter where you were, you were still the same old Jack, the same old boy, still your same old self?

The child's mother was suddenly there in the hallway, grabbing the child by the hand, and off they flew, so that the child was gone to church by the time the guitar salesman finally decided it was time to lie in bed no longer but sit up, for he needed to gargle the night taste out of his mouth. He looked at his undershorts, on which red thread had been stitched into lengths of script running completely around one hem:

> . . . time to wonder and to turn towards acacia
> blossoms white upon stones a hundred visions
> and revisions of simple blue paint dripping
> from a door . . .

And around the other:

> . . . in the sun for the world is always yours
> the evening heavier than the weight of all
> things that lying distant and alone . . .

He had not the faintest idea what it all meant. Words of the same style and unknown meaning were embroidered on the edge of a clean pillow slip that had appeared the week before, and the words *hemerocallis* and *japonica*—and others now forgotten except for what he vaguely remembered as possibly *casuarina* and *jessamine*—with their careful stitching were almost completely buried with a host of others in the yellowed terry cloth of his towel and washcloth.

He would not have mentioned these things at all if Mrs. Meuse from down the hall had not knocked with great complaint on his door, then impatiently pushed it open and asked him what she should do about her cat.

"What do all the words on the laundry mean?" he asked.

"Toes like a baby's," she said, "it's the trouble, Mr. Brockman. Who would have thought the lanolin to his toes was not what he would want? Who would have thought? Treat your pets like people," she said, "and they'll respond with respect. My, my, only ten o'clock and it's already hot," she said languidly drawing the back of one plump hand across her eyes and forehead in poor imitation of a prostrate Sarah Bernhardt. My name is Evelyn," and she gave him a long, satisfied look, "but I'll let you call me Eve if you so desire," she said, for Jack Brockman's fingers were long and delicate, his eyes an icy blue. It was impossible for women to see him and not wonder how it would be to have him in bed. "The poor pussy can hardly walk for shaking his paws and won't be happy and natural again until I can somehow wash it off," Mrs. Meuse went on. "But he won't let me do it now, doesn't trust me, I guess."

And Jack Brockman turned to grab his suit pants, as incidental to him—and as important—as a dowager's mink stole, for they were the only pair that he possessed, and went with Mrs. Meuse to hold her cat who, of course, was on to them both from the start and clawed a neat rip in the sleeve of Mrs. Meuse's pink Sunday blouse going down to the fleshy outer skin of her arm so that she bled in tiny drops, and Mr. Brockman watched her dab at these with a white handkerchief, which he saw had red script embroidered along its four borders.

"My cousin had a cat named Buckshot," he said to divert.

Mrs. Meuse dropped the handkerchief, for the cat scratched at her again, and Mr. Brockman picked the handkerchief up and gently pulled the white cotton out to read each of its four embroidered hems in turn:

> almonds in the palms of hands can they
> hear the tide against the shore hear
> the pebbles rock and sand almonds in
> the palms . . .

and then something about a wave—before giving the handkerchief back.

"What does it mean?" he asked.

"Oh that," said Mrs. Brockman. "I haven't the faintest!"

And he walked back to his room past Mary Catton's bucket with its mop left soaking since yesterday in lugubrious water, the old vacuum cleaner tank with sprawling hose and winding cord across the hall floor as if intent were equal to action, for Mrs. Zawinsky, the landlady, made a point of never asking anyone to do anything that constituted work on Sunday, not even the putting away of a mop. And he heard that gentle crying from the room above as he closed his door and took off his trousers to lie down again. Some repeated emotion of deep distress.

For the woman in the room above had wound down the same steep track of loss and regret since that night a month ago when the man she had loved had arrived later than usual. Now she tested and tried the scene over and over in her mind: the shadows from the streetlights resting on the sidewalk, the way he walked with her as if his thoughts were elsewhere. She could have guessed the worst: that his wanting to move on, the picture in his mind—so appealing and clear—of the other girl, the new one, had given him a distance.

"How long will you be gone?" she had asked.

"I don't know, Grete," he said, a lie—she knew—and yet she'd waited, breath held, for him to say something—anything—even that.

Standing in the grainy, dispersing gold of a streetlight she thought, Oh! He's telling the truth, and she reached out to him.

"Don't press me," he said.

The night weighed, for they were into August, and she smelled that sweet smell that was his alone, a thing she could not imagine living without, for love was one all-together thing to her: she had never learned to separate any one part of it from the rest.

"Good night," he said so simply and evenly that her heart, as if indifferently pushed, rolled out of its nest of young years and tumbled, breaking onto the sidewalk.

Now, over and over, it tumbled in her mind onto the same relentless sidewalk as she sat in her room by the window and picked, with her nail scissors, a line of red embroidery out of each side of the Peter Pan collar of her best silk blouse.

She had eyebrows and lashes that were so blond that the child—whenever she saw her teary face in the hall—thought they were invisible. Yet it gave her face, even in sorrow, a certain fresh and guileless look. Dusk, she thought, glancing toward the window, yet impossible to tell, perhaps a heaviness, a certain malady in the sky brought on by more bad weather.

This is truly the last straw, she thought, I will send my laundry somewhere else, for the blouse had come back with,

> love is a hard seed and memory relentless
> remember the stone the water and the star

embroidered in red thread around the lace edges of the collar. From above her on the second floor she could hear, as she picked at the red thread with her scissors, Mrs. Scharlach's daughter, who was in the midst of her weekly filial visit. As could the child, for it was early afternoon and church was past, and the child had been left to wander the halls while her mother sat in a parked car two blocks away with Jack Brockman, salesman of cheap Spanish guitars sold more for the indeterminate flowers like little perfect cabbages in brightly colored enamels painted on their bodies than for anything else.

The child needed no picture of what she heard through Mrs. Scharlach's door for she had seen Mrs. Scharlach often enough sitting in her wheelchair like a misplaced doll about to slide out onto the floor.

"I don't want to go," the old woman said, "I like it here fine. I don't know a soul there."

"You don't know anyone here either, Mother."

"Not true! Not true!"

"You only see people from the window."

"All the same I know them. If I was to disappear, they would want to know where I was."

And I too, thought the child, standing rapt by the door. I

would want to know where she was. Mrs. Meuse's door across the hall opened for only a moment, and the child saw a television screen and suddenly wondered if there were real people hiding behind those strange shadowy black-and-white characters, when Mrs. Meuse, seeing that the footsteps did not belong to Jack Brockman, changed her mind and abruptly closed her door.

Colonel Kramer, wearing a pinstripe suit in which the stripes were printed onto the dark fabric, causing there to be none on the knees and elbows where they had worn off, slept in his favorite armchair to the sound of a dense August rain falling against the side of the house. His monocle lay on his paunch, a silk handkerchief jauntily folded—but now wilting—was in his pocket, for he had decided years ago when a young man in Austria that he would always dress to impress.

As he slept he was a child again, and it was Sunday, the Lord's day; his mother and father had taken him visiting, and now it was dusk, and he slept through all the joltings of the road in his mother's lap. He could tell by the turnings how far they were from home, a last long, slow, arcing turn in which the horses trotted much faster as they sensed their beckoning stall, a last long, slow turn that seemed to arc in a great curve of deliciously prolonged pleasurable arrival. Then the wagon slowed to a gentle stop, the horses whinnied; there was a knock on his door, and he woke up.

"Colonel Kramer," the child said, "Mary is done with your shirts."

And she lifted to him a pile of newly starched shirts whose collars were too gray at the fold to ever come clean, but whose cuffs and front and back panels were now so ornate with red, embroidered script that they reminded him of peasant shirts:

> ... brittle-boned birds in the cradle of one's
> hand not with clubs the heart nor with stones
> whoever brought me here will have to take me
> home where hindsight is the only sight teach
> us for in the end one's tears are cried teach
> us to care and not to ...

and so forth and so on, so that each week when the shirts were returned to him the area of red embroidery had lengthened. He unfolded the top shirt to hang it in his closet and saw that the words had now begun to creep onto the shoulders.

It was a trespass, yes, but at the same time he couldn't deny that the laundress was paying him an attention of sorts. He felt not alone in this, for he had seen the same red embroidery on the other boarders' shirts and ties and vests—on, for example, the bib that Mrs. Scharlach's daughter used when she fed her mother. He had heard the old woman demanding that her daughter read the bib aloud in its entirety before tying it onto her. It was an embarrassment to be seen wearing the shirts in public, yet he knew if he complained he would simply be told by Mrs. Zawinsky, the landlady, that he could take his laundry somewhere else.

Colonel Kramer, breathless in the room's afternoon heat, which seemed more emulsion than air, returned to his chair and sat thinking about his shirts for only a few moments before an insidious, creeping fog loosened the fingers of both his hands, slackened his jaw and neck, turned memory topsy-turvy, and he slid back into the soft and grateful hole of his afternoon nap.

The child stood waiting by the door for her usual nickel, but the colonel's corpulent body and sweat-slick head had slumped into the chair as if all his joints had gently given up their part. The mysteries that were always present for the child when she saw anyone fall asleep seemed to tumble from his opening fingers to the floor. The moment had a sense of magnificence, and she thought, everything used to be something else and that something else was something else before that. At one time he'd been a colonel—or so he said—in the magnificent army of Austria. Now he was old and slept. Once, even further back, he'd been something else again, a small boy, even a baby perhaps.

While down the hall a woman that none of them knew, because she had just moved in the day before, could not be released from a vision of her X-ray in which the cancer had looked like a tiny star—something in Andromeda—as the light from the X-ray screen gleamed through it. One quarter of a centimeter, the doctor had said. She had not been able to take her eyes off it, could not move them away to the doctor's face. He was talking to her, telling her something, but she could not turn away from this tiny, growing point like a glint in the eye of a lover. For a moment she saw death as a boat crossing a wide body of still and murky water. But, no, hers was not like that. Hers shone with a fierce little burst of light saying: Here I am! Here I am! Try to catch me! Here I am! No wonder she'd read with special and desperate interest—as she looked for signs and messages everywhere—the red designs embroidered down the edge of each faded cotton curtain:

> . . . white dust of road scattered ashes the
> body of an old and curious saint like talc
> on the road who comes in white garlands
> invisible bearing nothing but the screaming

of the sun the cicadas of noon the clean
taste of fire in the wind mingled with the
taste of stone dissipates . . .

"Maybe it means I should not have the surgery, after all," she thought, though she was to see the surgeon in the morning and had come a long distance to be near a good hospital.

The child sat on the front steps, her face pink and swollen and languid after the rain, the steam off the slick, wet street like the smoke of woodland Indians that rises from a forest, the rejected crusts of a baloney sandwich in her lap. Her eyes seemed to disappear into their moist selves; her lids drooped; sticky brown curls clung to her head heavy with midafternoon exhaustion and the twilight that always lies between comprehensions. In front of her as she hardly sat awake, or hardly slept, Jack Brockman pulled up to the curb with her mother.

Sitting there in the car, they seemed at first like any ordinary couple to the child as her eyes opened and focused, Jack Brockman detached but irritated, the child's mother ignoring him but still completely wrapped up. The child looked at the car and then saw a palpable tension and felt that something was about to happen, something that would force one of them to get out of the car and shout angrily, slam a car door, walk away in haste.

It had started out as the usual and ultimately satisfying conversation having to do with their fondness, their friendship, their love for one another, the graceful shape and form—as the child's mother saw it—of their attachment. It had become a Sunday ritual, a conversation they played from beginning to end, not so different from the act itself. Yet for the child's mother it was even more important, for she could have lived without the other, so that when, in a free and easy way, he spoke, she was completely unprepared.

"It comes from your loving me more," he said.

"More?" she asked. "What do you mean by 'more'?"

"More than I love you."

He was completely matter-of-fact.

"Oh, come on," he said. "Don't go off on me now."

The child saw in profile his smile of assurance like a grownup explaining night and day to a child, and her mother's face, which had become vicious.

"One person always loves more than the other," Jack Brockman said. "You know that."

Jack Brockman turned and saw the child, started the motor, and the car drove off down the steamy street with her mother and Jack Brockman in it, and Mrs. Meuse walked down the front steps past the child, her cat restrained by a leash, the fabric of her yellow summer dress stained with moons of perspiration under her arms and below her breasts. And the child got up, for she felt that it was time to see if Mary Catton had laundry to be delivered.

"Last night," said Mary Catton, "I dreamed I was running away on a train."

She sat with a formerly white, unidentifiable garment in her lap that the child could see now had red script embroidery almost entirely covering it, the threaded needle held between her fingers, poised as if, for the moment, she'd forgotten it.

"I sat in the dimly lit train and looked out the window as I waited for it to pull out of the station. It was then that I saw the blind man standing on the platform, his stick white as neon, thin as a reed, and long as hope when it is still too young to know better. The station platform began to slide away, and the blind man's stick, a presence stronger than the man himself, slid away, too, and then—for I had to have been asleep to be dreaming in the first place—I fell asleep one more time, this time in my dream. One dream inside another like a gift box whose only gift is another slightly smaller box within."

She looked at the child who sat on the edge of the bed and seemed not bored, but waiting.

"Half-truths," Mary Catton said, "in which discarded bits and pieces float like memories along the tracks, bits and pieces over a world of unintelligible beginnings and misunderstood endings, things that should be kept, things that should be thrown away and no one to know the difference."

She remained silent then and took up her embroidery again, and for the child who knew Mary Catton it seemed the most natural thing in the world to tell one's dreams as stories, one's stories as dreams, for children are required to suspend disbelief all day and night long.

"I will have to begin ripping some of this embroidery out," she said. "There's simply no room left. This shirt will have to be a kind of palimpsest."

From the hall came the bumping sounds of suitcases, the disruptions of people stepping around the pail and mop, the vacuum cleaner in the shape of a bullet, the laudatory and imperious voice of Mrs. Zawinsky explaining that there were no meals on Sundays in deference to the help, though the child knew that it was because Sunday dinners were the most expensive to fix. The child got up and looked out Mary Catton's door and saw a man and wife with two very small children dragging behind them, tired and forlorn as children always are after long car trips.

The man had traveled a far distance and brought his family with him, because his mother, who was known to the child as Mrs. McNamara, had been taken to the hospital. In the morning they would all four pick up Mrs. McNamara and drive her back to the rooming house. They had come to do this, not because the man loved his mother—or even liked her—but because she was his mother.

"I've got cots you can use for the children," Mrs. Zawinsky said.

And the child followed behind them at a distance and watched the cots set up in old Mrs. McNamara's room, where each stem on the wallpaper roses curled and held each open, heavy blossom at the same precisely printed angle, their suitcases on the floor crowding everything together and taking on the dulled late afternoon color of shadows and dust as the man struggled to open the one window and found, when he had done so, that the room was still stifling hot.

The wife, with practiced stealth, removed a glass hip flask of gold-brown whiskey from her suitcase and shoved it under the mattress. Though the words *vicious cycle* had never crossed through her mind, the child recognized without a doubt certain signs of repetition and stealth. She saw, as soon as the husband and children turned their backs, the woman slip the bottle back out again and hide it under a large bath towel before she walked down the hall to the toilet.

The child returned to Mary Catton to tell her all about it, and the laundress gave her two hand towels to take to their room, two lovely, though slightly frayed, linen towels with red embroidery eloquently finishing their front hems. The first was a question that asked:

> will the nightjars remember to call each name
> inscribe it on the air

The second was a simple statement:

> stone is softer than hope breaks more easily
> under pressure of water

The last had been used by Mary Catton before. The child had seen it on her mother's garter belt, for these were the words—above all others—that the housekeeper found most universally appropriate.

The same words were embroidered down the interior seams of Colonel Kramer's vest as he slept in his chair and the languid sun slanted far and away beyond the house and over the rooftops of Minneapolis, making the spires and trees and Scientist Church's belfry into fantastic, stretched shadows so that it seemed those dense hours before twilight would never wilt but be imprinted in the bronzy heat forever.

Colonel Kramer slept in his chair all night long, because he couldn't breath lying down. He pulled himself to a stand with his cane and the edge of a table several times during the night to urinate into a mason jar, because he was too much asleep to walk all the way down the hall to the toilet.

Now as he dozed in the twilight, it seemed to him that the rain had started again, but then in his dream he saw that it was not rain at all, nor the thick leaves of dense windswept trees like so many hands clapping or waves breaking, but the two of them, he and Taska, clapping for a curtain call. The play was now over, and they sat in the packed audience, tired because they had worked all day but didn't want—no, couldn't—miss this one. They wore richly embroidered peasant costumes which gave Taska, sitting next to him with her brown hair braided in lovely green ribbon and tied atop her head, a sense of elemental dignity and pride as if she might, when they got home, make love to him on her own initiative without the usual artifice. But of course they'd never had peasant costumes, only seen that particularly intricate red cross-stitched work at certain country festivals when they'd been children in Austria.

The child sat on Mary Catton's bed and knew her mother would not be through with Jack Brockman until eight or nine—or even ten—o'clock.

"I was born in a manufacturing town called Cardiff," Mary Catton said. "We lived in the kind of place you see from the windows of a train just after it pulls out of the station. Those places are all alike, always the shades drawn. I wonder if travelers even think to imagine what goes on in those narrow rooms, the people that live there. My brother had a group of friends who stuck to one another as if their lives depended on it. They'd hang around, standing indifferently to show that nothing mattered and say there was no work to be done. It was their loose, transparent ethic revealing that everything mattered far too much. You know what I mean?" she asked the child.

And the child nodded just to keep Mary Catton going, because although she sometimes understood little, there were bits and pieces that made an imprint and came to life sometimes days later, bits and pieces that were retrievable and never got lost.

"The flush of dawn, for example, had lost all importance to them. They bore all the ragged thoughts of their young lives in their faces turned indifferent, in the way they held their heads back and to the side with arrogance, their glinting eyes watering with coal dust. So you see, one must try. Love is always the most sacred act." And she ran an absent-minded forefinger slowly back and forth over the texture of the stitches as she sometimes did over the cloth cover of a book she might be reading or the rim of a glass.

Mrs. Scharlach's daughter passed Mary Catton's closed door, trying not to think too deeply about her mother whom she had just fed, toileted, and put to bed, for the colored girl would be back in the morning to take over. She had mistakenly placed one of her mother's handkerchiefs in her pocket, and it stayed there silently bunched and waiting for her to discover it and read the four words embroidered in red, each across a corner:

>coral
>pink
>tourmaline
>bronze

which together—when she finally read them—reminded her of a sunset and had the effect of slightly elevating the feeling that life was too heavy to carry, a feeling that always overcame her when she visited her mother. She fell asleep that night remembering the drive she'd made with her mother to see the old house they'd both been born in, transferring her mother to the wheelchair in hopes that the chair would wheel over the tall weeds and grass, how the glass in the windows reflected the tops of the trees, their branches and leaves like memory itself, and then a square with no reflection whatsoever, and they knew that there a pane had broken out.

Mary Catton said, "This old rooming house is hardly just a house. If you were to dig around its foundation you'd be surprised what you'd find buried in the soil, sifting settling, leveling down all the time though you can't see it with the naked eye. The bones of sparrows and of mice, marbles like the eyes of little drunken gods among the lamb's ear and forsythia, a crooked fork, a liniment bottle, a diamond ring thrown out a window in the heat of an argument and searched for weeks on end but never found, layered under leaves the hollow stems of weeds and the base of a martini glass, screws and nails, the husks of bees. Neither houses nor people are as simple as we want them to be, and nothing is ever really forgotten or thrown out."

And the child saw how everything moves toward the next thing, how nothing ever stays in place, how beautiful and interesting everything was because of the imagination, even the ugly because of light. So it was with some surprise—because the conversation was seeming like a pleasant dream to the child—that they heard Mrs. Meuse's insistent knock upon the door and then Mrs. Meuse inquiring why the child was up so late and not at her homework for school, and where in the world was her mother, and the child saying that she was sure her mother would be along shortly but was still with Jack, and Mrs. Meuse's cheeks and nose turning the unpleasant color of half-cooked liver.

It was for this reason that Mary Catton suggested they find something small to embroider and place outside Mrs. Meuse's door. The child suggested a garter belt, but Mary Catton didn't have one and said that anyway a garter belt wasn't particularly appropriate, so they settled on a rather floppy and faded, slightly discolored silk rose that the housekeeper had saved off the shoulder of a dress. Though she thought the fragility of the silk would be difficult to work with, she nonetheless unraveled a strand of her usual three-ply red to only one ply, found a thin needle, and began to work.

So that when Mrs. Meuse later awoke thinking she heard footsteps, turned on the light and put on her robe and went to her door, she saw nothing but a rather morose flower lying on the hall floor which, when she picked it up, read in thin embroidery around its six petals:

> sit there where sky meets land sit and
> your chest curious and sorrowful as
> watch the colors change watch you heart
> happiness watch the curious glimmer
> a bundle of those things throbbing in
> of a thing there are no words for

And discovered through some experimentation, as she stood there, that the petals made more sense if read in a slightly different order. If it hadn't been for the thin red embroidery Mrs. Meuse would have done all she could to transport the flower in her mind into a token from Jack Brockman.

"You can see," Mary Catton said, "that when you touch the words with your fingers and let them stay in the dark night of your mind, they tend to flame out like brilliant desert flowers, like the midnight bloom of cactus. There are words one hears, things one sees, events of sometimes the briefest passing, that catch like a silver nail on the coat sleeves of one's heart."

It was so late that even the child thought of going to bed, though her mother was still not home, had certainly let the time get away from her as it always did when she was out with Jack Brockman, so that the child thought she might lie down on Mary Catton's bed, perhaps even move herself up and place a pillow under her head and sleep for just a little bit while Mary Catton worked.

Down the hall the new family lay in their beds and cots, and the father tried to sleep by remembering the old summerhouse garret enameled white, the ship's wheel that his grandfather had set up by the attic window so that his grandchildren, looking out over the ocean in the morning, could steer toward the rising sun in the morning and then steer their way home again at night. Under the shadow of the wheel, pulled by the moon into spectral elongation across the pine floor, and burning with the glow of long days on the sand, they slept in cots under the eaves listening to the sounds of night, the sullen ghostly foghorns, the buoy's muffled clang.

Yet this memory that lulled him into sleep, that played through his head as he dropped off in his own familiar house, now seemed, in his mother's rented room, to have no effect. He lay there in the dark listening to his wife and children breathing, smelling alcohol on her breath. He felt the mattress move when she moved and knew she was not asleep, then felt the mattress shift slightly one more time as she got up. The two-year-old could be seen in the moonlight with his thumb in his mouth. The three-year-old's head was obscured by a corner of blanket.

"Oh, my God, Joe," she said.

"What's wrong?"

She reached to uncover the little boy's head and saw his cheek glistening with spit. Still baby, he made a small whimpering sound like an animal, and his body moved in a small stretch.

"What's the matter, honey?"

"Nothing. He's alright."

"You thought one of them wasn't breathing again?"

"It's alright. They're both asleep."

"They're always only asleep," he said to comfort her. "And they always will be only asleep."

"You don't know that," she said.

He got out of bed to go down the hall to the toilet where over the sink hung a small rumpled linen towel completely covered with red embroidery so that—for a towel—it had an unusually rough texture. He put the toilet cover down and sat on it, then pulled the rumpled writing out flat so that he could read it before going back.

He lay next to his wife and heard from the floor above the gentle but incessant sound of a woman sobbing, and he repeated to himself in a whisper words he could barely remember from the embroidered towel:

"There where the roots of laurel and lime,"—something, something about ashes and love. "Of ash and love," he whispered, "a small white stone," but where, where was the stone? Where did it hide? he wondered, where was it? Ah, yes, he whispered to himself, "gleaming from a wash of rain and nesting in the hollows."

His wife had fallen asleep. Yet all that she desired as she lay next to him, that one small thing, had been impossible: the thankful gray nothing of dream-absent sleep.

The tears upstairs slowly diminished as Grete thought—with increasingly childlike expectation—that if one wished hard enough for something, someone to come back, for example, it was bound to happen. The power of wanting with one's whole being seemed suddenly not simply magic but efficacious and completely logical. Perhaps his leaving was only a step in some natural progression that—in the final analysis—would bring them forever and always together. She remembered her parents who had been—she seemed to remember—through the same sort of thing, always telling her that the course of true love never ran smooth, other people she had known, friends and acquaintances, legendary love affairs that occasionally ran off course, didn't Fred Astaire always lose Ginger Rogers before he won her back? I am, she thought, part of the human race. I have done nothing to be excluded from this part. But as she tried to sleep on her pillowcase, which read down its length,

> . . . primal elements remain no matter what the order . . . the words yes and no hello goodbye and air cloud breath . . . silver now gold and the petals of a mallow rose water and its direct opposite fire the retina of the eye stars night and dust on the road become a thin paste between one's toes . . . yearning and dreams the act of forgetting . . . resolve sudden unexplained fear in the night remorse wind earth pencil and paper and sky . . .

the certainty of his return dissolved into a kind of thin vapor that refused to stay fixed.

"The fading song of a mourning dove," Mary Catton said to the sleeping child as she turned out the overhead light, which left lit only the lamp she sewed by on the table, "even the rasp of a cricket, has more permanence than death, administers more comfort than love. I remember," she said, "how the street fell long and straight between the small brick houses, the way the light completely missed the street by two o'clock on winter afternoons as if the Lord had decided to withhold the street from his touch, the way the light always changed so that what it touched never stayed the same, how nothing is ever truly visible until the looking back."

And the child saw that it was the fine and delicate lines—those things easiest to miss—that sometimes held the most, that were sometimes in the end the heaviest.

Down the hall the woman with the cancer like a star lay in bed while energy and light streamed from a tiny point in her breast. Bright fragments of poetry floated in and then out of her head. For a while she thought they were original, that she had made them up, then she realized that she'd heard them all somewhere else, and she slept, dreaming of a blue balloon slipping out of her hands, lifting and floating until far up, far up and above, higher and higher and then even higher, it seemed pulled until it and the sky dissolved. Thin, indifferent clouds, like cotton pulled too thin to use, stretched across the blue, and she thought, it is no longer clear what will become of the day, as she rose in her dream from a bench and began to walk.

Mary Catton put down her needle and turned off the light. She had spent the day deep in embroidery, as she did every Sunday for no other reason than it was what she did when not laundering and cleaning and cooking and sweeping up the other six days of the week, that is to say, when she was not doing what she thought of as work.

She put on her nightgown and lay next to the child, for whom she had great hope in spite of the fact that the child's mother was most probably still with Jack Brockman and had clearly forgotten her. You are the child who has tied strings from me to other people and made paths in the tall grass, she thought, and she imagined the child with her tangled, uncombed nest of hair lying beside her as they slept.

All the house lay quiet now and so, too, Mary Catton, who said the words and phrases, lines and stanzas, in her sleep, for they were, to her, like paths the mind walks down because they're there, tears that slide down cheeks as rivers over land, each flowing in its natural course.

There was, as always, the sleep of dark colors, the dark images of cracked shoes, stale gravy congealed on chipped plates, and dung, paper bags blowing against battered brick walls in vacant lots, the stained ivory of piano keys, and the sound of music soaked like a fig in sherry with the strong taste of nostalgia, snow like handkerchiefs from the pockets of old men falling down the narrow street and melting into nothing as they dropped, her mother's eighty years that had weighed like little stones piled one atop the other on the bones of the old woman's shoulders.

Dawn came over the city like memory to an amnesiac. The child awoke, turned in the bed, opened her eyes, and saw Mary Catton sleeping next to her, dreaming a last shallow dream in which a man whom she had never met—but who seemed to her strangely familiar—looked at her with recognition as if all along he'd been expecting her, for his smile showed a small, private humor as if there were some shared joke between them.

Now every part of the room—the bed, the polished floor, the flowered bathrobe hanging from a hook on the door—reflected and rose together in the new light like parts of a new and startling song, for the whole room seemed to be a light description of something only just begun. Mary Catton's half-dreaming mind began to wake up, and the words appeared as if waiting in the wings on her lips. The world seemed distilled as though passed through some clear and necessary lens of crystal. An image formed in her mind, a thought. She could see it clearly and feel all that it meant in its simple being as she forced the words out of hiding to say the name of the thing to herself.

"Starling," she said, envisioning the slick wings tight against the body as it pecked the ground, the feathers seeded with minute oily spots.

Acknowledgments

The following stories appeared originally in these periodicals:

"Envoi" first appeared in *Mondo Greco*, "Travels in Arabia Deserta" in *New Orleans Review*, "Wheat Field at Auvers" in *Literal Latté*, "On the Night" in *Nassau Review*, "The Secret Life of Objects" in *Santa Monica Review*, "Fleurette Bleu" in *Georgia Review*, and "Provenance" in *Sewanee Review*.

About the Author

Photo by Vivian Gray

K. A. Longstreet, an independent writer, lives in Montpelier Station, Virginia.